The
Painters
of
Lexieville

The
Painters
of
Lexieville

SHARON DARROW

CANDLEWICK PRESS
CAMBRIDGE, MASSACHUSETTS

Copyright © 2003 by Sharon Darrow

First edition 2003

Library of Congress Cataloging-in-Publication Data

Darrow, Sharon.
The painters of Lexieville / Sharon Darrow. — 1st ed.
p.   cm.
Summary: Seventeen-year-old Pert Lexie does not think
things could get much worse in her small, impoverished
community, but when her uncle's advances go too far,
everything — including her determination to leave as soon as
possible — suddenly changes.
ISBN 0-7636-1437-8
[1. Family problems — Fiction. 2. Poverty — Fiction.
3. Country life — Arkansas — Fiction. 4. Snake cults (Holiness
churches) — Fiction. 5. Arkansas — Fiction.] I. Title.
PZ7.D2525Pai 2003
[Fic] — dc21   2002041142

2 4 6 8 10 9 7 5 3 1

Printed in the United States of America

This book was typeset in M Perpetua.

Candlewick Press
2067 Massachusetts Avenue
Cambridge, Massachusetts 02140

visit us at www.candlewick.com

To my daughters,
Kristen, Beth, and Stephanie,
and, with thanks, to my teachers,
Bret Lott and Fred Shafer

⮜ Jobe ⮞

BEFORE

Time was, nothing had changed, not for our whole lives. Rain in the spring turned our road to a bog, and I fishtailed it for fun down the ruts when I was driving in the pickup listening to the top country countdown, singing out loud, never seeing nothing coming. And Pert, she was a little girl, even if she was a junior in high school and looking like to be the first Lexie to make it to graduation. Orris was always picking on us, nothing new in that. And Papa, just trying to make a go of it with Mama getting quieter and stiller, though I hadn't yet seen it. I was just a boy then, though I thought I was a man.

Thinking back now to the day they found Orris, I can just about smell the damp pine needles, see the rain dripping off the end of a branch, and I can only stand amazed that any of us made it through at all. And what happened to Pert, whether it was grace or fate or divine indifference, is a question always in my own mind and, I suspect, will be ever' day to come.

❧ Pert ❧

A couple of weeks ago when my gym teacher, Coach Corder, announced this week's topic and told us who the teachers would be, I determined to steer clear. Mrs. Turnbull, the main Lexieville caseworker from the Spring County Welfare Department, and Katie, her helper, had volunteered to take mornings off to instruct us in the techniques of the Vernal chapter of the Arkansas Women's Self-Defense League. I'd managed to pretend to be sick for three days, and now had to hope they wouldn't recognize me and have to act friendly.

I opened the gym door and my ears filled with echoes, balls bouncing, rubber soles squeaking on the wood floor, and the bleachers clattering underfoot as the girls climbed up and sat down. But mostly the voices hit me, all high-pitched and giggly. And not one of them interested in whether I showed up or not. Except maybe Raynell, and she didn't count. Then came the whistle for roll call, and I had to join those girls all dressed like me in purple and yellow — the only time we all dressed alike.

When Coach got through the *K*'s and called out, "Lexie, Pert," I had to answer, "No shoes."

"Two demerits," Coach said. She squiggled them down in her book — one mark per shoe, I guess.

"Lexie, Raynell."

My cousin Raynell's pale little voice said, "Here."

I couldn't see where she sat, but I knew without me there she'd be all closed up, hands between her knobby knees to hide her bitten-up nails, flimsy hair screening off her face from the girls on both sides.

Brittany Lee Hathaway and a couple of her followers jostled each other around on the bench, their shiny long hair pulled up for class, ponytails bouncing and flitting all around.

Coach Corder blew her whistle. "Girls, let's get to work. We'll let Mrs. Turnbull and Katie take right up where they left off yesterday."

Mrs. Turnbull, in a navy blue sweatsuit, her frosted hair in a curly bob, looked as neat as she did in her office suits and skirts. Katie set up an easel and an orange posterboard sign. The poster said:

1) STOMP INSTEP
2) BACKWARD KICK TO THE KNEE
3) JAM NOSE WITH HEEL OF HAND TO NOSTRILS
4) PULL EYELIDS

Just reading it made me shiver. But *oohs* and *aahs* and a few giggles rose from the stands.

Mrs. Turnbull looked up and smiled. "Now, girls, let's get serious," she said. "Remember, this is not a laughing matter. This is about defense, not revenge."

Katie and Mrs. Turnbull stepped onto the mats and pantomimed stomps on each other's feet, backward kicks against kneecaps, and all the rest. The girls laughed and took it all in like a show.

When they got finished Katie called out, "Are there volunteers?" Brittany Lee jumped right up, of course, knowing what to do and how to do it.

Mrs. Turnbull scanned the bleachers. "Any more volunteers?"

I put my head down and tried to disappear. Mrs. Turnbull hooked and reeled in three or four girls for her demonstration, and I sat up to watch. But as I straightened up good, Turnbull got me in her sights.

She pointed at me and jiggled her hand up and down trying to think of my name. "Lexie," she said, and waved me over to her group.

My socks slipped a little on the wood floor, then sank into the mat.

Mrs. Turnbull described the moves to us, said how we should be resourceful in our self-defense. "If the aggressor tries to carry you away upside down, pinch his inner thighs. And pinch hard," she said. Katie nodded.

Mrs. Turnbull put a hand on my shoulder. "Now for the backward knee jab." She looked at me. "What was your first name again?"

"Pert," I said, and looked down. On the mat my white socks had the pale orangey stain of Lexieville dirt on their toes.

"Pert," she said, like, *Oh, yes, now I remember.*

How she'd gotten so far along in that County Welfare job and still not know any better than to recognize a person in public was a wonder to me.

"Pert, try to grab me from behind."

I pretended to grab. She pretended to rear back and kick out my kneecap, then we switched places.

Mrs. Turnbull and Katie chose more girls until the whole class got a turn, even Raynell, all red in the face. When class was almost over, Brittany Lee got the job of demonstrating the use of keys, pencils, nail files, and other household items in case of a sneak attack. Katie finished it up by saying, "And always tell someone."

Mrs. Turnbull put up another posterboard sign, one

with a drawing of a determined but happy-looking girl. She pointed at her and ended the whole show by saying, "You have a right to put boundaries around your own body. It is yours. If you ever have cause to use these methods, defend yourself. Don't be a victim."

That picture girl had dotted lines drawn all around her body, like a case to fit into. No wonder she smiled. I'd never imagined myself like that, with an invisible picket fence around me nothing could get through.

When the bell rang, I figured I'd learned just about everything I needed to defend myself no matter what. And I knew what that girl in Mrs. Turnbull's picture knew. Courage was the main thing.

I slid across the floor in my socks. Everything sounded and looked better: the voices echoing, the mats being stacked up, the floor shining golden, and the sun cutting through the tall windows onto purple-and-gold Sardis High Swamp Cats banners. I belonged to myself.

In the locker room I dressed in my jeans and a new navy blue T-shirt Jobe'd gotten free from the auto supply store where he did odd jobs every once in a while. He'd let me wear it first. The color almost made my eyes look dark blue, and the thick cotton still had the dye smell in it. If I held my notebook just right, no one had to see the square white letters spelling out *Engine Joe's Motor Parts* across my chest.

When I got to math class, I opened my book and tried to get to work, but I hadn't counted on Brittany Lee up in the front row making so much racket. She crossed her legs and kicked one foot, making the tassels on her shoes jingle, the only sound in that quiet room besides pencil scratching.

School used to be okay before BLH and those other Vernal town kids moved out here in junior high. Not long after she moved here, I heard Brittany Lee say something under her breath to her best friend, Mindy. I caught the word "trash" about the time they both cut their eyes over at me, then seeing me watching, sat and studied the lettuce and mayonnaise oozing out from their thick pink ham sandwiches. After that it got like she smelled me or something.

When the bell freed us from math class for lunch, I was more than ready.

I went through the cafeteria line and got my lunch tray, unable to hide the stiff white vinyl letters on my shirt while I carried it. I had to walk past Brittany Lee to get to my usual table on the other side of the cafeteria. Not talking, me and the other girls from Lexieville hurried up and ate our best meal of the day. Every so often we looked up to see if anybody noticed us, but no one paid us any attention. Over here in the corner, we knew our place.

The other Lexieville girls looked just like me: secondhand faded jeans in a style a couple of years past, no-name athletic shoes, our hair doing whatever — too straight, too curly, too oily, too limp.

But there was one thing that set me apart. Now I had that picture in my head of the girl safe inside her boundary lines, and I planned on getting out. Some of them might have the same idea, but some sure didn't.

One of them who didn't was Raynell.

Raynell was the oldest of seven children by who-knew-how-many fathers. Gloria, her mother and my father's niece, still hadn't even gotten around to naming the last two kids. We all just called them Boy and Little Sissy.

Raynell squirted another packet of mustard on her corn dog, and it struck me that I had to get away from *her,* like if I didn't get up and out of that lunchroom right then, I'd never get out, never get away from Lexieville.

I jumped up to take my half-empty tray back. But something made me stop, lean over the table, and warn her. "Raynell," I whispered, "you better wake up or you're going to end up just like your mother."

Raynell looked up, a smear of mustard on her upper lip, then tears came into her brown eyes. Now I'd done it.

9

I walked away, emptied my tray into the garbage, and stuck it on the dishwasher conveyor belt.

Outside, I closed my eyes and leaned against the warm brick wall of the school building, trying not to see Raynell and her mustard face. She should just be glad I cared.

SPRING COUNTY WELFARE DEPARTMENT
HOME VISIT FORM

SOCIAL WORKER: Alice Turnbull   # SC 7

CLIENT: Gloria Ellen Lexie & family

ADDRESS: Lexieville Circle (4th house on right)

PURPOSE: Follow up and investigate elementary school teachers' concerns over the condition and health of the younger children.

FINDINGS: In my early afternoon visit, I found their clothing in piles on the floor, old food scraps and mouse droppings in the kitchen cabinets, and the two youngest children splashing in the muddy yard. I awakened Gloria, who was dressed in rumpled clothes that appeared to have been worn for some time.

RECOMMENDATIONS:

- *Gloria (32):* Life Skills and Job Training — 12-week program (mandatory).
- *Sissy (5) and Boy (3):* Enroll in preschool Early Start program.
- *Raynell Louise (17), Cody Michael (14), Rhonda Lee and Ronnie Lee (twins, 11), and Will (9):* Confirm all enrolled in free breakfast and lunch program.

FOLLOW-UP:

Family: Monthly drop-in home visit.

Gloria: Biweekly office visit and counseling session.

⇒ Pert ⇐

The bus rocked up onto the asphalt from the school driveway. We turned south on Valley Road between the paper company's tall skinny pines and drove on through the blotchy shade to the scraggly part where they'd planted new baby trees to replace those already cut down. Low sunlight flashed through the pine tree rows. At the crossroads just past the bait shop–gas station– convenience store, Sardis's only business, we turned onto the gravel road toward Lexieville. A few yards down the slope, the gravel disappeared into muddy ruts.

We bounced hard. Five or six rows in front of me, Raynell tipped off her seat and nearly fell into the aisle. I was glad I'd avoided sitting with her, which turned out to be easy, since she got on after I did and squeezed in with some of her brothers and sisters instead of coming back to our usual seat. She could go ahead and be mad. I didn't care.

Out the window a damp smell rose from beneath the tangle of brush under the huge old trees just leafing out and all covered with twisty vines and brambles. It wouldn't be long till the bugs and snakes'd start stirring under there, too.

Lexieville was not like a real town with video stores, pizza places, car lots, churches, and all, but just a bunch of houses squatted down on low ground about two miles from the two-lane at Sardis Crossroads. The rutty dirt road went past Lorelei Childers's white-painted house first and then ours, which had been red once upon a time, then led to a sort of dusty clearing in the pine woods, with maybe eight or ten other houses set around it, depending on which ones still stood after a rain, fire, or flood. Most of the old wood houses people hadn't ever painted at all, though they patched them up with scraps the flakeboard plant threw in their dump out here not too far from Lorelei's place.

Today a couple backhoes and a Bush Hog worked in a lot next to the dump, clearing it for something new, an unusual sight in Lexieville. Maybe the rumor Lorelei was spreading could be true, that some church people from Vernal were starting up a mission out here. Why they wanted to come out here was a mystery to me.

If I could be headed in any other direction, any-where but toward Lexieville, I sure would be. In a little over a year I'd be the first in my family as far back as we could remember to end up with a high school diploma, and I'd be looking to put it to use.

Papa always told me, "Keep on with your schooling and graduate, Pert. We'll keep you fed till then." He'd look right into my eyes with his soft gray ones. His frown lines would deepen, and he looked old and wise. "You got a head on your shoulders, and if you use it, no telling what you can make of yourself. No need to drop out like Jobe or to start looking for a husband." Even with him trying so hard to look strict, I knew how much he loved me.

He told me, "Time was, I thought I might get that diploma and make a better life for your mama and me, but it weren't to be. When my daddy died, and with his brother already gone, there was the nieces and nephews to get raised. Soon y'all came along, and, what with your mama getting poorly, my chances just passed by. Now I'm afraid Jobe has lost out, too. I don't aim for that to happen to you."

I didn't need much more encouragement. I'd shake the dust of Lexieville off my feet as soon as I could. I might even change my name, manage to get away from people who heard "Lexie" and thought they knew all about me and my kin. I planned to use my grandmother's maiden name when I lived in town. Trish Trahern would go over better any day in a place like Vernal than Pertrisha Lexie.

The bus rocked from side to side, passing along in front of my house. A few patches of red paint still showed up under the eaves. Long and narrow and just two rooms deep, it was what they called a shotgun house, except ours didn't have a covered porch out front, just a low step. And there on that step sat my mama, Truly, and her younger brother, Orris. They were laughing at some private joke.

The bus swung around the circle of Lexieville's unpainted frame-and-flakeboard shacks, and the kids' shouts got louder, their scuffles rougher. We gathered up our notebooks, stood up, and pushed into the aisle. When Raynell got off the bus, she ran with the other kids without a backward look. I stepped down into the mud, then cut through the nearly bare trees and bushes, their tiny yellow-green leaves just starting to bud, hoping I could sneak around to my back door without Orris and Truly catching sight of me.

I reached our yard clearing just as Orris raised a brown longneck beer bottle, his Adam's apple sliding up and down as he swallowed. Then he gave it over to Truly for a swig. She tipped it up and drank.

Her face looked extra pale in the springtime sun. Her freckles, nearly invisible all winter, were starting to stand out from her skin.

She spotted me and hurried to tuck the bottle down between the two of them.

"Hi-dy, Pert," she said, and wrapped her old beige sweater tight around her. "School out?"

I almost asked how she'd missed catching sight of that big yellow bus bumping past in one direction then back in the other not three minutes ago, but I kept my teeth together.

"Yeah," I said, still heading for the back door.

Truly waved a bunch of wildflowers at me. "Come on over and say hello."

Orris stood and hiked up the waist of his faded jeans. "Here," he said to Truly, "give me a few of them flowers to give to Pert."

I hurried on, but he caught up with me about halfway to the back door.

"Here," he said, and shoved some bent-over wild daisies in my face.

I wouldn't take them, so he grabbed my hand and forced it open. He clamped my fingers shut over the damp stems. "Now say, 'Thank you, Orris,'" he said, his voice all singsongy.

Up close the changes time had marked on him stood

out. His whiskers were sprinkled with white now, and his eyes, too much like my own pale blue ones, had gone faded and watery, almost clear.

I tried to pull away, but he squeezed my hand so hard pain shot up my arm. I wanted to see that girl in Mrs. Turnbull's drawing, dotted lines like a fence surrounding her, protecting her. But it was no use. Here in Lexieville, it was just me and Orris with nothing in between.

"Thank you," I said through clenched teeth.

"Thank you, Orris," he repeated, his breath puffing against my cheek.

"Thank you, Orris," I mumbled back.

But he couldn't let it go at that; he had to point his grimy finger at me. "You think you're too good for your own family? I'm here to tell you, you ain't nothing, Pert Lexie."

Heat poured over me. I backed away and, when I was far enough, threw the flowers at him and ran in the back door. I slammed it, locked it, shot through the kitchen into the front room, and, dodging our beds, went for the front door, meaning to lock it, too. But it opened.

My knees almost gave way then and there, but it was only Truly coming in, sniffing at her bunch of wildflowers.

"Pert," Truly said, her voice stretched thin and high.

17

"What's the matter with you? You hurt Orris's feelings just now." She pushed her hair back off her face, and her frown lines deepened.

"I did not." I looked down at our unpainted floor-boards. "I'm sick of him. And I don't want any stupid flowers from him."

She rubbed her forehead. "I got such a headache." She took off her sweater. "When he was a boy, he was a sweet little thing. Brought me flowers." She whispered, "Still does."

The silence in the room sat between us.

"And a bottle," I said.

Truly took the wilted flowers and put them on the windowsill by her and Papa's bed. She didn't say anything back, so I'd know how bad it was to say that about the bottle. She gazed out the side window, her shoulder blades punching out the thin cloth of her faded blue cotton dress.

Early twilight, pale orange, came in around her, and she and it and all in the window were the very colors of sorrow to me. At first I wanted to yell at her, then I just wanted to hug her, but all I could do was say, "I'm sorry."

Her whole body relaxed, like she'd been waiting on those words all her life. She put her forehead to the glass and murmured, "Sometimes, in order to get along, you got to go along."

⁓ Truly ⁓

I've held my forehead to this pane so long it's no longer a refreshment, no cooler than the spring evening air. Outside there's just pine trees, scrabbly stones, thin weeds, and pinecones scattered like lost children.

The pine needles stir, and the windowpane clouds over with yellow pine pollen.

Water's running in the kitchen — Pert's putting on the kettle, clattering a pan around, letting me know about it.

Deep down I feel her and Orris reaching out to me, both needing something only I can give, but I can't figure what it is. It just makes me so tired.

I'll lie down awhile, ease back on my bed so's I can rest and look out my window, enjoy through the yellow pollen haze the swaying pine boughs, green against the sunset.

⇻ Pert ⇺

After Truly settled down on her bed for a rest, I opened a can of vegetable beef soup for our supper, put it on the stove, and went to sit on the front step to try to do my math homework. But mostly I stared down into the red dirt with its little yellow rocks and struggling clumps of new grass. I rubbed my sore hand and imagined a scene where Orris lay out in Lorelei Childers's front yard, kneecaps smashed, hollering out in pain, Lorelei dialing for an ambulance.

In Lexieville, nearly everybody was named Lexie, except Lorelei, and since Orris lived with her, I figured that almost made her a Lexie. Lorelei owned the land under Lexieville, and she also leased the dump to the flakeboard people. All the tenant women living on welfare back in the woods around Lexieville wondered what she put up with Orris for, anyway. She had some money and could afford this and that to make herself up with. She probably could find herself another man, if only she'd kick out Orris and crook her little finger in another direction.

I couldn't help but wonder what she wanted with a man like Orris. A while back when I'd gone over there to borrow a aspirin for Truly, I'd said, "What you see in Orris, anyway?"

Lorelei, in her yellow-and-lime-green flowered house-dress, her black ponytail tied up in a real fluffy red scarf, leaned back in the kitchen chair she'd put in the shade of her big pine tree. She stared up into the top branches. Looking up that way, her double chins all stretched out, she was a pretty woman.

She thought a minute then started in. "I remember well when my daddy bought these acres and we left out of Fort Smith, about a year after my mama died. I was fourteen, and Orris was about seventeen at the time. Daddy'd hired him to help repair the chicken coop out back. One night when Daddy left to go on about his business, he told Orris to stick around and told me to get him a beer. After that, Orris sitting out on my front steps drinking my daddy's beer got to be a habit. One night I sat down beside him and said, 'I know the only reason you come here.'

"He said, 'What's that?'

21

"I said, 'The beer my daddy lets you drink.'

"'Pretty good reason,' he said, and winked at me.

"Then my heart went fluttery when he leaned over and whispered, 'You could give me a reason besides the beer if you wanted to, Lorelei.'

"He gave me my first kiss, then he laughed and said, 'Reckon Lorelei is better than beer?'

"I'll never forget the way he said 'Lorelei.' Then he kissed me again and said, 'I love you.'

"And I remembered what my mother told me when I was twelve and had matured: 'The first man to love you, Lorelei,' she said, 'is your heavenly mate.'"

Little tears sprung up in the corners of her eyes. "Why, Pert, he was the handsomest boy, what with his blue eyes and the way his hair fell down over them." She shook her head and looked at me. "Just like yours does."

I'd hurried on home that day and dug around in my mama's button tin until I found some hairpins. I pinned back my bangs and declared I'd never let them down in my face again.

Now Papa and Jobe drove into the yard, and I nearly jumped out of my skin when the horn honked. They climbed out of the truck dressed from head to toe in white. The two of them looked like skinny angels.

Jobe, his gray eyes all round and bright under his white cap, looked more awake than I'd ever seen him.

I went out to the truck to meet them. "What in the world is going on?"

Standing proud, Papa said, "Jobe and me, we got a job." He took off his cap and slapped it on my head, grinning.

With an all-new look in his eyes, Papa — a working man now — winked at me as he reached back inside his door for a small paper bag.

"A job, what kind? You bakers or something?"

Jobe and Papa looked at each other and laughed.

"Mrs. Turnbull has made us into painters," Jobe said.

"Painters for the county," Papa added. "We're going to paint any county office or courthouse room that needs it. She finally got us the job she promised."

Just over a year ago, a couple of months after Jobe quit school in the middle of his junior year and made Mrs. Turnbull mad, she'd said, "Mr. Lexie, you and Jobe and Orris may have to start working for your benefits." Papa and Jobe, they'd hoped for any kind of job the county'd see fit to hand them. But Orris, course, he was a different story.

"What about Orris? Does he get a job, too?" I wanted to know, thinking that might keep him away from here, even if he didn't deserve it like Papa and Jobe did.

"Yep, and he's supposed to get hisself in there tomorrow and let the county set him up with brushes and paint, hats, shirts, pants, even new white socks, like she did us." Papa lifted up his pants leg and showed off his new socks, just as white as they could be.

Jobe glanced at me. He hated Orris, too. Orris always punched him in the stomach to check if he'd grown any muscles there yet. Now Jobe grinned, took his cap off, smoothed his sandy hair, put his cap back on, said, "Mrs. Turnbull's one Orris knows better than to mess with."

Papa laughed, and we practically danced through the door, but he hushed as soon as he saw Truly laid out on her bed. A hint of beer hung in the still air. Papa glanced away, his lips a thin line, and we went into the kitchen, where he took a box of RodentOut! from the paper bag he'd brought home. "Let's see if we can't get rid of some of them mice your mama's been fussing about," he said. He poured some of the white powder into a Mason jar lid, set it and the box under the kitchen sink, then made himself a cup of instant coffee with the water I'd heated.

"What we having?" he said, and checked under the lid to see what was cooking.

"I just opened up some vegetable beef," I said.

Once Truly woke up, we were in a celebrating mood again. After supper we sat on at the table and talked, excited for what it appeared life had dealt us.

But Truly seemed almost more proud for Orris than for Papa or Jobe.

"You pick him up now, John. Don't forget," she said to Papa like she thought he might, and laid a freckled hand out on the table next to him.

Papa patted her hand and stood. "I won't. We're going to need all the help we can get, working for Mrs. Turnbull." He and Jobe grinned at each other and got up to put themselves to bed early for work.

Workers, our men were workers.

I stayed up late, doing homework at the cracked oilcloth-covered table in the kitchen's dim light while Truly washed up the dishes humming a little. The splash and hum from over there made me sleepy till I finally gave up and laid my head on my math book. It smelled like school and pencils.

Truly shook my shoulder, whispered, "Pert, get on in to bed." She smiled, her face looking more like it did when I was little.

I stood and shut my book on my papers. We hugged, my arms up over her shoulders, me the tall one now. For the first time in a long while, we just hugged easy and fine, neither one of us needing special comfort from the other, needing it and not finding it.

⇜ Truly ⇝

I know it's a dream, but I can't wake myself. Time after time, I pull Orris up onto the big flat rock where we went to hide out from our papa. I know he's taken another beating in my place, and I rock him till finally his cries stop and he snuggles down to sleep. Then I walk out in the moonlight and it's clear nothing is as it was, nothing as it should be. Trees that I've known since childhood are gone, and huge old ones stand where our house should be. Where the road was, it's now a river, deep and swift, eating away the banks, and the water is purple from some hidden light. I turn and run, but my legs won't work and the water comes nearer and nearer. Voices cry out, and I see Pert and Orris trapped out there on that big rock with no way to shore except for them to step into that roaring flood. Water rises on the rock, and Orris, my brother, pushes her in. Pert whirls by just out of reach, staring at me, her eyes holding me, like she thinks I can save her. But I can't. I wake myself up crying out, and John covers me and pats on me, but I don't think I'll ever go back to sleep.

⇜ Pert ⇝

Next morning, after Papa and Jobe left for work, I dashed out, sliding in the muddy road to the bus stop. I couldn't wait to tell Raynell our good news. If she wasn't still mad.

At the bus stop, Raynell appeared not in her usual jeans and T-shirt but in one of her mother's miniskirts and a pair of white flats already caked nearly to the brim with red mud. She'd never worn dresses, not even when she was a little girl.

She pretended nothing was unusual. I almost laughed, but something uneasy stirred in my heart.

"Pretty shoes," I said.

Raynell said, "Thank you. They're some of my mom's." She looked down, said, "Durn it," tiptoed over to a patch of grass, and tried to scrape the mud from the sides of her shoes. "I wanted to look good today."

I started to say, "Give it up, Raynell," but I didn't dare. She had me a little shook. Yesterday she got all mad when I compared her to her mother; today she'd dressed up like her.

I told her about the painting, and then the bus came and we climbed in. She must have forgiven me, because she took her place beside me and, like most mornings, slept till we got there. Some nights, 'specially when her mother'd gone out partying, she didn't get much sleep and tried to make it up before we got to school, though I'd seen her nap through her classes plenty of times.

We bounced and rolled up onto the asphalt, then turned in at the gate in front of the elementary school, and the bus half emptied. On down the drive, past the playground swings and stuff, we let out the middle schoolers, then around the football field and track we finally stopped at the high school's side door. All the Sardis schools sat in a long row, all on the same property, all in the same yellow brick that Vernal's clay pits had become famous for.

"Raynell, wake up," I said, and bumped her with my elbow.

She popped her eyes open and looked out at the school for a second before she gathered herself up and stood. "We're here," she said.

We stepped down off the bus and slipped unnoticed

into the noisy stream of blue-jeaned legs and bright shirts, shouts and laughter, toward the lockers.

Raynell waited for me while I struggled with the combination. She stuck her spiral notebook between her knees, got her comb out of her jacket pocket, and used her freed hands to comb and smooth that dull, straight hair of hers, pale yellow, the color of winter grass.

❧ Jobe ❧

This evening Raynell walked by all dressed up in a skirt and everything, and I thought she must be going somewhere, so I went out there and said, "You need a ride in the truck?"

But she said, "No, Jobe, but I thank you anyway. I'm just out to enjoy the spring air."

We stood there struck quiet a minute, but neither one of us said, "Well, I better go," and soon we got to talking.

"It'll be so good when school gets out." Raynell puffed air out her lower lip and made her bangs ruffle, like it sure was hard work.

"I'm working now, regular with the county," I said. "Mrs. Turnbull's put us on."

"I heard," she said.

"Pert tell you?"

She nodded her head. "Yeah, and Mr. Nunn, next door, laughing about how Mrs. Turnbull got Orris's goat again, this time making him show up and wear them painter's things. He says she does it every chance she gets. Says ever'body else's give up on Orris, but not Mrs. Turnbull. She's going to hound him till he gives in or dies."

We laughed, then somehow got around to talking about where Gloria'd gone off to tonight, and Raynell said, "She's out looking for Prince Charmin' again, but you'd think she'd figure out by now there ain't no such of a thing."

She squinted up at me, and all I could think about was Cinderella before her godmother got ahold of her with a magic wand. I knew for sure I didn't have no magic nor nothing, but I wished I did. All of a sudden, she quit being just Gloria's oldest kid, hanging around Pert all the time, and turned more real or something. About that time, Pert came scooting up beside us.

"What?" she said, looking back and forth between Raynell and me with this funny look, like she was getting left out of something important. I popped my fist against her arm and she popped me back, only harder.

⇜ Pert ⇝

Back off the road between our house and Lorelei's stood our chicken coop and outhouse. When we were little kids, Jobe and I'd found a little clearing farther on back, hidden by trees and underbrush. It became our own secret place. When the new spring leaves on the vines thickened up and hung like a blanket over everything, we liked to scoot out there and rest in a nice shady spot under a big old oak tree until our mama missed us and called, "Pertrisha, where you at, girl? Jobe, come here and help me out," and we had to go heat up water for the washing or burn the trash.

For over a month now, Orris had gone to work regular. So I wasn't worried about running into him today after school when I went back out to the clearing to get away from the heat of mid-May built up inside our house and study for my math final.

The sun'd dried up the ground enough for me to sit awhile. I settled my rear end down between two of the old oak's roots that fit around me like armrests, and leaned against the bumpy trunk. Those yellow-green leaves rattled around above me in a breeze I didn't feel at all down here. Darts of sunlight hit my eyes along with peeks of blue sky and made me want to breathe deep and drink up that blue air like water.

The bees got to humming, and the earth warm and tangy smelling. I got drowsy enough to nap. When I roused up, the shade had crept long and low across the ground. The underbrush blocked my view of both our chicken coop and Lorelei's house. All of a sudden it seemed too quiet. No birdsong. Even the breeze had stopped. Way over in the circle a dog barked, sharp, three times, and I heard a rustle behind me. I tensed and leaned forward, trying to see around the tree.

Orris. Right there not ten feet away. I bolted up, feet sliding in the pine brush, and ran. But he got me. He grabbed me from behind up under my arms and tried to tickle me like in the old days, his fingers jabbing the sides of my breasts, and his whiskey-sot breath on my cheek.

"I got you now. I got you good now," he said, and laughed like this was some kind of game.

I opened my mouth to yell, but he pulled me closer, wrapped one arm around my middle, and clapped his other hand over my mouth. His palm stunk of dirt and oil and covered my nose so tight I couldn't breathe.

I tried the backward kick, jabbed at him with my heel, but I couldn't find his leg. I couldn't get a breath, my head got dizzy, my chest ached.

I twisted from side to side, the trees swinging around, whirling around. He slid his hand off my mouth and jerked my chin toward him. Then his mouth was on mine. But instead of his usual quick scratchy beard peck, he kissed me hard and I got real still, my eyes staring into his. For a second we both got scared. He stopped, still holding me too tight. Then he looked at my lips, pressed his mouth on me again, and moved his hand from under my arm to my front. I tried to scream, but my voice stuck in my throat.

I opened my mouth wide as I could. And I bit down. Hard.

I tasted something warm and wet and thick.

Orris flinched and loosened his grip. He swiped at his tongue, then checked his fingers for blood. Gasping and panting, spitting and spewing out his blood, I saw my chance. I grabbed his eyelids with my fingers, pinching and gouging at the same time.

He hollered.

I tried to yell, but my voice came out in a whisper. "Orris, I'm going to rip them off your face."

I meant it, and I knew I could. But he got his hands around my wrists and squeezed. My fingers went weak and let go just as he brought up his knee, hard and quick, into my stomach. It threw me all the way back under the tree.

I pushed myself up against the tree and held on. I said, my voice hoarse now, "I swear if you don't go away, I'll tell."

Orris came closer. His teeth pink from his bleeding tongue, he said, "Who you going to tell? Your mommy? Or maybe your friend Mrs. Turnbull? Ain't nobody going to believe you."

Real steady, so he'd know I meant it, I said, "I'll tell Lorelei."

He stopped and stared me down, his face so pale the whiskers stood out against his skin.

"You'd better stop, Orris."

He knocked me over and sat on my legs. His hands pressed my shoulders into the ground. His face close to mine, bloody mouth hovering over me, he said, "Say, 'Please, Orris.'"

Pine needles pricked my back and a stick jabbed my thigh. I twisted away, and my hand felt for it. Not a stick, but my sharp yellow pencil.

Orris licked the blood off his lips, and his mouth came toward me again. He went for my neck and his beard scratched deep.

I bent my arm at the elbow and, with all my strength, stabbed.

The point hit resistance, then ripped through the thin painter's pants and sank into the soft skin of his hip. He caught his breath.

I pulled out the pencil, went again, and buried it even deeper this time. He hollered. I let go.

Orris jumped up, hopped around, touched that yellow pencil, touched it again, not quite able to pull it out, like a cowboy trying to get up the courage to pull out an arrow.

Laughter, high and howling: me, a crazy person. That pencil looked so funny. Orris's hopping around looked so funny. I laughed and rolled over onto my stomach, and got up on my knees just as my mama came crashing through the brush.

"Orris Lexie, I declare. . . ." Truly shook her head like she didn't know what to think when she saw that pencil.

Orris, one hand behind him on the pencil, pointed at me.

But she didn't look at me. She said, "Orris? Why aren't you at work?"

He pointed at *her* then, and jabbing his finger in the air with every word, he said, "You just shut up."

I ran for home.

Truly followed right behind me, and when we got to our outhouse she reached out and held on to my arm, her fingers rough and pink. She said, "Whoa, explain yourself."

I took a breath, and my heart quivered. "You better tell him to leave me alone."

Her face pale, her freckles little islands across her nose, she leaned against the rough gray boards. "He was just playing."

"I don't like that kind of playing," I murmured, tears coming up in my eyes.

I pulled away from her, went inside the outhouse, and latched the door. I heard her footsteps go toward the house. I figured I'd given her the headache so she had to go lay down again.

Quiet now, I listened for Orris. Nothing from the clearing in the woods, then a yelp of pain. He'd pulled out my pencil.

Late afternoon light filtered in through cracks in the old boards. I put my eye to one, peered out. Nothing but trees and just a part of my house. If Orris ever caught me again there was no telling what he'd do, no telling what *I'd* have to do.

The ugly sharp smell of the outhouse rose around me. My stomach rolled. I lifted the wooden lid and threw up into the pit. My stomach grabbed and grabbed till past empty. Weak, I leaned against the wall.

A vehicle out on the road. It passed Lorelei's. A fender rattled. Then it turned in at our house and pulled up onto the thick carpet of pine needles and parked: Papa's truck. I walked as fast as I could, my legs wobbly beneath me.

"Papa," I called, and caught hold of him before he could grab off his hat.

"Hey, Pert," he said, and tottered, me nearly knocking him off balance.

He smelled like paint and fresh air.

"What we celebrating?" He laughed and pulled back to look at me. He stopped grinning and said, "You sick? What's the matter?"

He looked right into my eyes, and I came this close to telling him I'd stabbed Orris. But I didn't. No way could I tell him something that might change the way he looked at me.

I swallowed. "I'm not feeling too good," was all I could say.

"Did your mama give you the stomach medicine?"

"No. I didn't ask her for any."

Jobe got out of the truck and showed me a can of

leftover paint with pale blue drippings around the rim and a stack of newspapers.

Papa said, "Read them if you want to, then tomorrow you can help your mama out with the papering." He reached for a plastic bag on the truck seat. "Got some mousetraps, too." He turned away from me and headed for the house.

Before I could stop myself, I said, "Papa, I need to talk to you about something important." I held my breath.

He looked back at me. "What is it, Pert?"

Truly creaked open the door. Maybe she was going to tell him. But her eyes, round and sad and waiting to see what I was going to say, made me shiver.

I let my breath out. "It's nothing."

"You said 'important.' We better talk about it." He stepped back and waited.

So I came up with something to say, something I just realized could get me an early start on the road out of here, away from this life: "You think I could get me a job in town this summer?"

Truly's face relaxed. "Y'all stop fooling around and get on in here for supper."

Papa looked at me like he hadn't seen me in a long time. "A job. I don't see why not." He smiled big.

"How do I go about it?"

He got real serious and rubbed his chin. "Well, I'll tell you, it's right hard. Places you'd want to work at don't want to hire you, and half the time places you don't want to won't, neither." He shook his head. "You just got to go around asking if maybe there's some work for you, first one place, then another."

When he went in, I sank down on the steps to try to read the papers. I *would* be fine. I'd just keep taking care of myself. I'd get me a job.

Next day, I knew Truly and I'd set out the mousetraps and make new shelf paper for the kitchen cabinets, then tack up crisp, clean news all over our front-room walls, where it'd keep the flying bugs out. She'd tell me to take the funny papers for my corner and put the sports pages behind Jobe's cot. She and Papa'd have the brides and the houses for sale. But she'd never again speak of what had happened with Orris today.

I tried not to care, tried to read about the world out there: which fish were biting on what bait on whatever lake, where the president'd sent his army to feed some starving children, how much I saved myself every time I cut my own hair with the school art scissors, plus who from around here had gotten married, dead, born, or put in jail.

And right then, right there, board by board, I built

41

my imaginary boundary fence. Like armor made of solid wood, it started about six inches out and curved and shaped around me, a case to hold me, like a wood-carved girl.

It was past dusk now, the woods across the road black and full of sound. Crickets, cicadas winding down, and the racket the frogs made down near the creek somewhere: loud and soft, loud and soft. I listened to all that life out there, nearly every inch crawling with creatures. Some called out to let you know they were there; some slid along and kept quiet. The hair rose on my neck at the thought of faded blue eyes watching from the deepest dark under the trees, and I hurried inside and latched the door.

SPRING COUNTY WELFARE DEPARTMENT
HOME VISIT FORM

SOCIAL WORKER: Alice Turnbull   # SC 7

CLIENT: Orris Lexie

ADDRESS: Lexieville Rd. (1st house on left — Home of Lorelei Childers)

PURPOSE: To follow up on my telephone call inquiring into Orris's absence from his job as a painter in the county service. His excuse, a fall from a ladder onto a broken paint-stirring stick, could not be corroborated by either Jobe or John Lexie, his coworkers.

FINDINGS: Orris Lexie must have seen my car approaching, for he came outside about the time I drove up. He was unkempt, his gait was unsteady, and I suspected he was inebriated. He purported to be in great pain and unable to return to work for some time. I told him I would have to give the job to someone else. At that point his anger flared, and I left the area.

RECOMMENDATIONS:

· Orris Lexie's position as a painter will be terminated, and another recipient will replace him.

FOLLOW-UP: His file will be reviewed quarterly.

⤝ Pert ⤞

Already mid-June, school out two weeks, and I'd had
no luck getting a job, so once more I put on my
job-hunting clothes — a denim skirt and T-shirt — and
hitched a ride with my papa and Jobe on their way to
check in with Mrs. Turnbull. They let me out at the
courthouse, where lawn sprinklers splattered green grass,
old trees, and little red-and-pink flowers all the way up
to the white limestone walls. The clock on the top
whirred, then played a nice tune when it struck eight
o'clock.

Jobe and Papa waved and called out, "Good luck,"
as I crossed over to the drugstore on the corner, where
I planned to drink a soda and wait for a while. When
the businesses opened up, I made my rounds again.

My hair'd grown almost long enough to tuck around
back of my ears, and I'd set out to get a job working in

town the day after school let out. I put a yellow pencil behind my ear and a smile on my face, but nobody would talk to me about working for them down in Vernal at the movie theater, Dairy Bar, or any of those whoop-de-do hair salons. I walked, talked, and filled out applications, but nothing had worked.

No luck again today and at three o'clock, I turned down a street of two-story white frame houses with porches and hanging baskets full of flowers. The sidewalks and street covered over with tree branches made a tunnel of slanty shade to walk through. An old redbrick office building about two blocks away was where I was headed. Up worn stone steps, then I went in and told that college girl, Katie, "I was wondering, could I see Mrs. Turnbull?" and she let me go right on in.

I walked down a hall that could use a new coat of sunshine-yellow paint to an office where the door stood open, went in, and waited by the desk. Mrs. Turnbull waved her long hand toward a chair for me to sit on, her fingernails filed into smooth ovals and painted clear. Her hair, like the ads in the paper, curly and bouncy, looked natural, but I imagined it took a hair salon a while to get it like that. She probably had to go all the way to Little Rock for that kind of quality.

"Hello, Mrs. Turnbull," I said, my mouth all dry and pinched up. *Howdy* was easier to say, but I knew where

I was and what I wanted. I didn't want to get off on the wrong foot with an idea so good she'd wish she'd thought of it herself.

"Hello, Pert," she said.

I took a breath and said, "I guess you didn't expect to see me here this afternoon."

Mrs. Turnbull propped her chin on her clasped hands, two fingers steepled there in front of her nose. "How may I help you, Pert?"

I laughed and spread my hands out so she'd see how simple it would all be for her. "Here's the thing, Mrs. Turnbull. I've looked high and low for a job in town, and I am telling you, they are scarce."

Mrs. Turnbull looked at my hairpins and the pencil over my ear, as I went on about trying to get a job at the beauty parlors, where I thought I could do a good job for them. "I've been cutting my own hair for years now, Mrs. Turnbull, and with school scissors, that's saying a lot."

"Well, I never." She looked at me like she'd never seen cut hair before. "Pertrisha, if you want to be a hair stylist, you have to go to school to learn how."

I smiled. "Well, I need a job today, so I got to thinking. About the painting? I could help my papa and Jobe out." I spread my arms wide again. "They've already told me about stirring and mixing and washing down the woodwork first. Some days they get pretty short-handed, and I said to myself, 'Why don't I go down there and offer to help y'all out?'"

Mrs. Turnbull shook her head. "I am sorry, but painting is a job set up for the men — though I must say some of them are doing better at it than others. Orris, for instance, has turned out to be a bit of a disappointment."

My mouth got dry. I smoothed my hands down over my skirt, tucked it in under the sides of my legs, and said, "Yeah, I heard about his accident."

"A paint-stirring stick," she said in almost a whisper. She glanced over my hair, clothes, and shoes, but her eyes kept coming back to the yellow pencil I had tucked behind my right ear. She leaned toward me, full of feeling for her duty. "How else can I be of help to you, Pertrisha?"

I sighed, my shoulders rising up and falling down heavy. "I want to help myself," I said, "by working, saving up, and then" — and here was a new idea — "maybe sending myself off to Little Rock to hairdresser's college after I get out of high school." For a second I felt the itch of tears.

She propped her chin back up on her steepled fingers and pursed her lips. She just sat there and stared at the yellow pencil.

Finally she looked into my eyes, straightened up, and leaned toward me. Right then I knew we had an understanding between us.

"How about this? Since it seems like we have an opening, why don't we go down to the storeroom and find you some paint clothes?"

She smiled like the two of us were in this together. "Then, if you do a good job working with your father and brother, we might see fit to help you go to beauty school when you finish high school."

She said if I went away to school in Little Rock I'd live in an apartment and meet lots of young women my own age. She told me all about Little Rock, talking for a good quarter hour about schools and jobs, malls and offices, more people than ten Vernals. She still had friends there, had gone to college right there in Little Rock herself, said UALR had night classes, and maybe someday I'd think about taking some. I laughed at that, but she didn't seem to mind.

She led me to the closet at the far end of the hall and helped me search out my sizes in boxes full of white painter's pants, shirts, and hats. I put them on right over my clothes. On my way out, she straightened my hat, gave my hand a shake, and told me where I could find Papa and Jobe to give them a big surprise.

When I walked into the courthouse ladies' room in

my white clothes, not a speck of paint or dirt on them yet, and said, "Surprise," all I could think was I wished I had a picture of this. It was the first time I'd ever noticed how much alike they were: Papa and Jobe turned at the same time, paint rollers dripping, and had the same what-in-the-world look on their faces. Papa whistled, smiled, and said, "Well, howdy-do." Jobe laughed, slapped my back, and handed me a brush full of snow-white paint.

"Don't worry," I said, "long as you both do what I say, we'll get along just fine." They laughed.

When it was time to go home, we drove out the highway, then off of the gravel road to the two-rutted dirt track that led through the sandy bottoms back into the woods. Papa honked the horn, and a car parked at the flakeboard dump pulled out fast and headed back to town. A truck unloading cinderblocks in the mission lot beeped as it backed up, and at Lorelei's, we passed Orris laid out fast asleep, hands crossed over his chest like a dead man, Lorelei beside him on her old red chair. Papa honked and woke Orris up. Orris got up on one elbow and glared. Papa and Jobe just laughed but that frowning picture of him lingered behind my eyes.

Then Papa and Jobe and I waved our hats out the windows and rode around the big dirt circle of unpainted shacks, dogs and kids skittering out of our way.

Our neighbors and kin looked up like they wondered what'd hit us. When they saw those three white hats, they straightened up from feeding their chickens or checking the oil up under a car hood and either gave a wave back or frowned and shook their heads like, *Who does John Lexie think he is?* Boys and girls, Gloria's bunch among them, ran after us, tried to grab ahold and jump on in the back. A couple of them hopped in and waved at everybody with us. Papa drove us around the circle and around again. We honked and hollered and waved our hats. We wanted to see and be seen. We were the painters of Lexieville.

One more time Papa drove around the circle, then turned for home. We bumped up into our yard, over ruts and chug holes that made the front fender rattle even louder than usual. I reached over and honked the horn a last long blast, and Truly came to the door.

"What is going on now?" she said.

Jobe got out. "Pert's a painter with us," he said across the hood. "Mrs. Turnbull fired Orris and hired Pert."

Papa, already out of the truck, reached into the back for the leftover paint. "Yeah, we got us some help now," he said. "And here's a little dab of the bathroom white I thought we might could use somewhere."

Truly said, "What about Orris? What about when he gets better?"

Papa stopped and looked at her, then went on around back with the paint bucket in his hand. Jobe and I looked at each other through the windshield.

"Orris still needs a job," she said. She crossed her arms, her gray eyes sharp and hard on me.

I stepped around her into the house.

Then she reached up and grabbed my hat by the bill and took it off, just like she would Papa or Jobe if they tried to come into the house with one on.

I held out my hand till she gave it back, then took and hung it on a nail in the wall above my cot.

✒ Jobe ✒

That Pert, she'd done surprised us all. Got herself hired on, and didn't do no half-bad job, neither. Papa seemed proud, both his kids working side by side with him.

Things was going pretty good, us working days, then coming home and watching that mission house go up. Raynell heard tell they'd likely use snakes to demonstrate how much faith they had. Her and me figured that'd be worth seeing, maybe even dropping a dollar bill into the basket for.

❧ Pert ❧

After a little practice painting, you'd think I'd never done anything else. I'd gotten the hang of it right off, 'specially with Papa and Jobe both giving me instructions. They had a system, and once it was taught to me, we worked like a team painting the county clerk's new shelves. That clerk was a woman, so she didn't raise one eyebrow to see me painting with the men.

I got the job of painting shelves up high on a ladder, Jobe in the middle, Papa floor level. I tried to see how smooth I could make the brush strokes. The bristles made grooves in the thick paint, then the wet surface melted together. This was not such a white white as the bathroom paint and not so shiny, just right for shelves. The paint smelled clean and serious, and when the brush was full, it slipped over the wood like thick cream.

We talked only when necessary and only in quiet tones. After all, people sat working at desks in the rooms to our right and left, typing and answering phones. From listening to one-sided conversations, I got some idea about the work the county clerk had herself doing: handing out birth, marriage, and death certificates. She must give all that information to the newspaper, I figured. And the sheriff just added the jail part.

For lunch we went by a little store, found a picnic table across the street in the city park, and ate sandwiches we made out of crackers, cheese, and thick slices of log bologna. When we finished, Jobe and I leaned our backs against the table to watch the squirrels dart around in the splotches of shade.

Papa stretched out on the other bench. "I'll catch a couple of winks," he said.

Pretty soon he was snoring, and we laughed. The courthouse clock struck the half hour. Jobe turned around and put his head down on his arms. I watched the traffic for a while, then walked over to the water fountain.

A car pulled up and beeped the horn. I jumped. Wiping water off my chin, I looked up. Mrs. Turnbull waved me over. She had a passenger I almost thought I ought to know but couldn't place. He rolled down the window so Mrs. Turnbull and I could talk.

"Hello, Pertrisha," she said, and when she said it, the boy looked closer, like maybe he knew me, too. "How was your morning at the county clerk's office?" Mrs. Turnbull asked.

"It was just fine, Mrs. Turnbull. So far I have painted brick, metal, and wood. I like wood the best."

Mrs. Turnbull nodded. "So you're enjoying your work?"

"I am," I reassured her. "Painting is the perfect job for me."

The boy smiled. So now I looked at him straight on. About my own age, he had brown eyes and blond hair long on his neck and somewhat in need of a comb. His lower lip on one side got a little lopsided when he smiled — and I recognized him.

"Elwayne?" I said.

He laughed. "Hey, Pert."

"Elwayne, is that you? I haven't seen you in a long time."

He smiled and nodded. "I've been down in Texas with my mom."

I started to ask how was Texas, but remembered I'd heard not long ago he might have been in reform school somewhere down there and that his daddy'd taken this up with Mrs. Turnbull. Now here they sat in the same county car together. I guess she'd come to his rescue, too.

"I see you two remember each other." Mrs. Turnbull waved her smooth white hand at us. "Did you go to elementary school together?"

We nodded and looked back at each other.

Elwayne said, "It sure is nice to be back here."

Papa and Jobe came up behind me, and I moved over so they could lean down and speak to Mrs. Turnbull.

"Afternoon," Papa said.

Jobe took his turn. "Afternoon, Mrs. Turnbull."

Then they saw Elwayne and welcomed him back. Papa even reached in and patted him on the shoulder. "Bet your dad's mighty proud to have you home," Papa said.

Elwayne nodded.

Mrs. Turnbull said, "I have some county work for Elwayne, so you'll be seeing him around a lot this summer."

Elwayne waved at me when they drove away. I felt better than I had all day. I guess Jobe could tell, because he looked at me funny. Papa didn't notice.

Jobe said, "I bet we won't get much work out of you the rest of the day."

I laughed, but I made sure to work extra hard so Jobe wouldn't tease me later. That evening when we finished the shelves and washed out our brushes, I went home tired but happy. If Papa were to ask me what I remembered best from this day, I'd sure know what it was.

On our way down the road to Lexieville, just across from Lorelei's, we caught the first glimpse of the new church building taking shape, just the framing out of the floor, wood all white and fresh in the evening light. We slowed down to get a good look, then Papa said, "There's your mama. Over to Lorelei's."

Truly and Lorelei stood out by the road watching the hammering. Orris sat on a pillow in a lawn chair by the house, his bare feet propped up on an ice chest. He hadn't shaved for a while and up under the arms of his dirty T-shirt, yellow patches showed. I could almost smell him.

Lorelei and Truly came over to Papa's window. Orris leaned forward in his chair and yelled at Papa, "Some fool's putting in a damn church."

"It's the First Send-the-Light Gospel Church mission," Truly said. "We talked to the ministers, the one from town and the one for out here."

"They's Holy Rollers, that's what," Orris growled.

Jobe whispered out the side of his mouth, "He wouldn't know a Holy Roller from a hole in his head."

"They was wonderful men, I tell you," Lorelei said

with her hand over her heart, "and they want us to be their helpers to invite others to see the light before it is everlastingly too late and to worship together for the first time in Lexieville history."

I wanted to laugh out loud: Lorelei, a missionary woman.

Truly, two bright spots showing on her cheeks from all the excitement, lifted up her chin. "Reverend Blankenship, that's the missionary to here, said his wife is looking forward to meeting the ladies from Lexieville and getting to know us."

Papa smiled. "That'll be mighty fine," he said. "Jobe, you climb on in the back and let your mother ride home with us."

Truly got in beside me. If she'd already decided to join up with that church, she could forget about wanting to take me along. Papa'd lose out, but I didn't have to worry about Jobe: he'd keep me company.

I went to bed that night and took some time to mull over my day, thinking about what would I do if Elwayne happened to drop by for a visit. I'd just got to the part where he took me into his confidence and started to tell me what'd happened in Texas when I overheard Papa telling Truly how she needed to spend more time with me, of all things. I paid attention.

"I been noticing she's as tall as some of them office

women and as big, too. You need to show her some things; like now, half the time she wears Jobe's clothes."

"Pert don't listen to me about things like that," Truly said.

I nearly groaned out loud. She'd never even talked to me about things like that.

"Elwayne Nunn's boy, Elwayne Jr., was brought back here by the county. I guess ol' Elwayne finally got something on Belle to get him away from her."

Truly clucked her tongue. "Who would've thought someplace in Texas could be worse than here?"

Papa stretched and turned over. "I guess I'd better find out what that reform school stuff was all about."

"That's their business, John," Truly said.

"Not anymore," Papa said. "Not after the way he looked at our girl."

After a week or so of seeing neither hide nor hair of Elwayne Nunn, I decided to visit Mrs. Turnbull during my lunch hour and casually ask after his health. Maybe I'd find out where she'd put him to work and happen to drop by there sometime.

Well, no need for all that. I walked in the Spring County Welfare Department and nearly ran right into Elwayne cleaning the inside of the frosted-glass door with a rag.

He straightened up ready to start a conversation. "Pert, how you been?" He was all smiles.

"Elwayne!" I said, real surprised sounding. My face got hot like it might be a little pink, and I hoped it didn't show up like Jobe's. "Mrs. Turnbull been keeping you busy?"

He nodded and shrugged. "Better than sitting around, I guess."

It got quiet in there except for the fan whirring above our heads and Katie typing on her computer behind the reception desk.

"Has Mrs. Turnbull planned what you'll do once you graduate?" Welfare office business was as good a topic as any.

He shrugged. "We haven't gotten that far along yet," he said. "Right now I just want to stay in one place for a while, and it looks like Lexieville is going to be it."

He couldn't have said a worse thing for our prospects together. "Well, I want to leave Lexieville more than anything else I can think of," I said, meaning even romance.

About that time, a woman in a business suit arrived and Katie picked up the phone and said, "Child welfare is here." Mrs. Turnbull brought out a little girl, still hiccupping from a big cry, and handed over some paperwork. Before she let go her hand, she patted the girl's head and whispered something to her. The little girl nodded and took the child-welfare worker's hand.

Elwayne looked at me. A trembling seemed to come from his middle, and his voice quavered a little. "Maybe her mama don't want her."

"It's probably not that bad. If her mama's like Gloria, she just gets all stressed out, can't handle it, runs off, gets some free time with her kids safe and sound at the welfare foster care, and comes on back. No big deal."

Then I finally got it. "Elwayne, did something like that ever happen to you?"

"Not exactly."

"What then?" I said.

"I don't know, I guess I thought my dad didn't want me, is why we left and went to Texas."

After a few seconds I asked, "What happened down in Texas?"

"Guess me and my mom just couldn't get along. I took a car and got sent to jail. My mama ranted and raved, said, 'I give up on you,' and washed her hands of me."

He laughed — one of those laughs you use when something isn't funny. "I told her, 'Who gives a shit?'"

I struggled between the words he said and the feelings I caught coming through them. His hurt hit me in the gut. "I'm sorry, Elwayne."

"Hah, don't be. Getting away from her was the best thing could happen."

Seeing he didn't want my sympathy, I asked, "Why'd you steal it? Didn't your mom have one?"

"Naw. So while she and her boyfriend were locked up in her room, I borrowed his car." He shrugged. "I didn't count on them having a fight and him leaving early. He got so mad, he told her they were finished and called the police." He looked down at his hands. "She blamed me, said I made her lose the only good thing in her life."

I said, "He wouldn't just say, 'Forget it,' when they put you in jail?"

"He wanted to hurt my mom, and anyway" — Elwayne frowned and looked out at the street — "him and me didn't much like each other. I wasn't too surprised."

"It's not fair," I said.

Elwayne turned and looked straight at me and said, "Pert, you want to go to the Fourth of July fireworks with me?"

My pulse fluttered. "Okay," I said.

"We'll have to catch a ride with somebody," he said, and laughed. "I don't think I want to borrow no more cars for a while."

* * *

When Jobe and I pulled up in front of Raynell's house the evening of July fourth, Elwayne ran over from his dad's place.

We bounced down the ruts out of Lexieville, through Sardis, and on over to the Vernal city park by the lake. The parking lot looked like all of Spring County had shown up. Jobe drove nearly to the last row to get a space.

"Meet back here when they're done," Jobe said, and he and Raynell went off to find an empty tree to lean up against.

The townspeople had spread out on their lawn chairs and quilts, some eating bucket chicken and drinking from cans. Elwayne and I looked at each other. My face heated up and I shrugged. "Where you want to get?"

Elwayne took my hand and led me through the crowd back to the fence between the park and the woods. We sat down against it, and soon twilight settled in to full dark. The first flares shot up, lighting up the sky. Voices *ooh*ed and *aah*ed, and Elwayne and I joined right in. He leaned closer. "You having fun?"

"Yes," I shouted over the next blast. Elwayne stuck two fingers in his mouth and whistled so loud I had to cover my ears. He flopped back against the fence, and the chainlink rattled against the posts on either side of us. I leaned back and found Elwayne's arm a cushion between the fence and my back.

"How's that?" he said.

"Just fine," I whispered. His arm around me made me go quiet and still inside, but alert in the nerves just under my skin.

Elwayne put his mouth close to my ear. "That was a pretty one."

I leaned toward him. "Yes," I said in his ear.

Through whistles, gasps, claps, even when somebody's baby screamed at the loudest boom then settled in and cried, we sat like that and talked whenever the least little thing occurred to us. When the fireworks stopped, the sky seemed empty with only the stars, and them so far away. And Elwayne and me — it was like we were floating in the softest, darkest part of it.

The picnickers shone flashlights and gathered up their things, then shuffled along the edge of the lake back to the parking lot. Coolers bumped their legs, lawn chairs clattered, and children slept on their shoulders. We sat on in that dark. After the car engines and tires across gravel quieted down, frog croaking started up and we could hear little waves lapping against the shore.

"Do you think we should go find Jobe and Raynell?" I said.

"Not yet." Elwayne's voice soft, he wrapped both

arms around me. I liked the warmth from his body and the tickle of his breath against my cheek. He wanted to kiss me, I knew it, but behind my shut eyes Orris's face suddenly appeared — his stubbly whiskers, his nasty eyes.

I tensed.

Elwayne drew back.

Disappointment started through me, then someone coughed nearby.

Elwayne got still and looked toward the lake. I turned, too. A dark shape moved away from a tree and into the open. Orris! I sat up.

A lit cigarette dropped to the ground and went out. The click of a lighter. A spark. An orange flame rose from waist to mouth. The flame lit the face, and it was some stranger, not Orris at all, staring into the flame.

Then came the sound of footsteps through the grass and Jobe's voice. "Hey, Pert, is that you?"

The man snapped the lighter off. The moon's light took over and shone down on Raynell and Jobe, coming toward us.

Back at the truck, Elwayne and I got in the cab beside Raynell, me on Elwayne's lap. Elwayne noticed how shaky I was and held me tight.

Jobe turned the radio on loud, and we bumped up and down through the parking lot to the highway. Raynell put her head on Jobe's shoulder, and Jobe held her hand.

The dashboard light shone on their intertwined fingers —
his long and thin, hers small and sturdy.

We turned at the stoplight in the middle of Vernal,
drove past the Food Center and Sonic, and sped into the
darkness that surrounded Lexieville, while damp, woodsy
air blew in the window and big fat bugs splashed on the
windshield.

≫ *Truly* ≪

As that mission church gets built up, I feel more awake
than in a long time and go sit out on the front step
to enjoy the morning light and listen at the hammers,
their echoes pounding through the trees, and the scream
of the saw rising above them. I never noticed it before
the Blankenships came, but the main difference between
Lexieville and anywhere else was no church house.

When Lorelei and I go over to see the progress,
Reverend Cusper Blankenship says, "Watch out, here
come miracles, just prepare ye the way of the Lord."

He says the Good Lord will show us signs the
likes of which most of mankind have never seen nor
will ever hope to see. He says the saints will raise up
vipers in their trusting hands and never be hurt. He
says it's fearsome and sometimes even he is sore afraid,

but he does what he must. He's been called. I look in his steady eyes and know before me stands a mighty man of power — one like you could wish your son'd grow up to be.

These days, the three of us, Orris, Lorelei, and me, we all do find it a fine pastime to bide awhile and watch the work on the mission building. I was anxious to see what the paint colors would be in case they'd have any excess, but so far only white and brown, it looks like. The county has a better pick of colors for my flooring, and I'm thankful for that. I've taken one of Pert's pencils and drawn a patchwork pattern right on the floorboards for John and Jobe to follow. The fresh smell of paint and the brightness it brings my whole room makes me feel like there's so much about the world to look forward to enjoying. Surprising what just a little something bright and clean can do for the soul.

Sometimes, when there's nobody anywhere around, I get the buckets with just the paint dregs left, and a couple of small brushes, and get down on my nice bright floor and go to painting. I can make the shapes of things I see around me, but of course this being wall and trim paint, I don't have the colors that things call for. I like it, though, that a tree can have yellow-and-purple bark and peach-and-blue leaves, that the stream can look like a sunset, and a sunset like colored glass. I let them dry and look again later to decide whether to keep them or just paint them over with a block of solid color. Most times, I just paint them over and go on.

⇜ Pert ⇝

By late in August, Elwayne and I had gotten to know each other pretty well. Almost every night after I came home from painting and he got off from the county road-weed cutting crew Mrs. Turnbull had transferred him to, we ate supper, did any chores we had to do, got ourselves washed up, and strolled over to the skeleton shell of the First Send-the-Light Gospel mission. Builders had been working all day nearly every day, and soon the roof'd go on, and it'd be all done.

Tonight, Reverend Blankenship'd put up a big tent on the building site and started a revival meeting. Up between the new wood rafters he'd hoisted a big vinyl banner: *PRAISE and GLORY WELCOME WEEK!!! COME and BRING a FRIEND!!!*

I sat down on my front step to wait for Elwayne, already missing the warm sawdusty smell of the mission and trying to think of a good place for him and me to pass the time. Just about sunset the heat eased up a little, and the day's haze settled down between the trees and me and the road. In the quiet, a chirp or a rustle out in the trees got my attention every once in a while.

"Pert," Elwayne called, and I jumped a little. He walked toward me from the shadowy road, wearing his green T-shirt and jeans, his blond hair looking more combed than usual.

"Hey, Elwayne," I said. I went to meet him. Something stirred in me, something deep down and good. I thought of a place we could go — the big flat rock where Truly used to take Jobe and me when we were little to lie on our backs and watch the stars fall.

I led him by the hand to the path into the woods. We wove in and out the trees, brushing against pine needles. By the time I found the rock we could hardly see it; the dark was thickening around us.

Feeling with our hands, crusty lichen rough under our fingers, we climbed up. We sat close together, the black sky above us full of icy white stars. Elwayne slipped an arm around me. I put my hand up to his and we twined our fingers together.

I slid my other hand around Elwayne's neck, and I pulled his face down to mine and kissed him.

I wanted to laugh and dance like I'd just won a prize,

71

got my chance at something I'd been afraid I might not get. We kissed again. For a minute, it was like I was some other Pert.

An all-new feeling spread from him through me to the inside of my skull. Smooth, a smooth then trembly warmth, started low, spread out, down my legs, and up into my lungs.

His beard, just a little grown out since morning, scratched my cheek. I tried to keep my mind away from how Orris's whiskers had scraped along my neck.

I turned my head and shook it, my eyes wide open. But I couldn't forget. Just like at the lake, cold ran through me, and I pulled away from him.

"Do you mind if we go back now, Elwayne?" I whispered.

"Course not," he said, his voice thick. He got off the rock and helped me down. We walked a ways not saying anything, like we didn't hardly know each other. I hated Orris, how even when he wasn't around he could mess everything up.

A few minutes later, Elwayne and I stood on the road in front of my house. Amplified piano music and voices floated toward us, singing, "Hallelujah, Thine the glory, revive us again."

I said, "What do you want to do now?"

Elwayne said, "We can go spy on those church people.

It'll be fun," but his voice sounded sad. "We can just watch from outside. We won't go in."

I let him pull me down the road toward the music and the yellow light, the white tent lit like a lantern. They'd rolled the flaps up tight around the top, and between the poles we could see rows of chairs almost all filled.

The people who'd driven in from Vernal had on some nice clothes, more colorful than those worn by the folks I recognized from here. Raynell was there with Boy and Little Sissy. I spotted Lorelei. And there beside her sat Papa and Truly. Papa appeared to be enjoying himself, and Truly looked to be already under Cusper Blankenship's preaching spell.

Cusper raised his arms and his voice. "Will He spew you out of His mouth? Or will you, yes, you right here in Lexieville, and Sardis — *Sardis,* brethren — Arkansas, be given the Morning Star?" He paused.

Cusper's wife, Pansy, played some "Hallelujah" chords. When she hushed, he stalked over to the pulpit, grabbed up his huge black Bible, held it high above his head, slowly lowered it, then reverently opened it near the end.

He thundered forth: "'He that hath an ear, let him *hear* what the Spirit saith unto the churches.

"'And unto the angel of the church in Sardis write:

These things saith He that hath the seven Spirits of God; and the seven stars; I know thy works that thou hast a name that thou livest and art dead. . . ." Cusper stopped and glared. His disgust moved like a wave across the crowd. He stood and stared them down until they tucked their chins and lowered their eyes.

He whispered into his microphone, "'If therefore thou shalt not watch, I will come on thee as a thief, and thou shalt not know what hour I will come upon thee.'" He paused, got even quieter. "Thou shalt not know.

"'But,' he shouted now, thrusting his hand in the air, "thou hast a few names *even in Sardis* which have not defiled their garments, and they shall walk with me in white: for they are worthy.

"He that overcometh, the same shall be clothed in white raiment; and I will not blot out his name from the book of life. . . .'"

Cusper, pausing, seemed to gather his strength or maybe try to keep himself from crying. He whispered, "'He that hath an *ear,* let him *hear* what the Spirit saith unto the churches.'"

Elwayne whispered in my ear, "Only ones in Lexieville dressed up in white's you, your papa, and Jobe." He laughed. "And Orris."

I didn't laugh. None of that struck me funny.

We stayed on until we'd watched four or five get religion, one of the first being Raynell. She set the two little ones down and there she came, head hanging, creeping down the aisle. That was more than enough for me. I wasn't about to stand there and watch any more. I ducked away from Elwayne and headed across the road into the trees that skirted Lorelei's yard. He followed.

"What'd you think of that?" he said when he caught up with me.

"Elwayne, can we just not talk about it?"

We walked deeper into the woods, then cut across the clearing toward my house. We didn't talk at all until my back door.

Elwayne touched my arm. "I'm sorry, whatever I did."

"You didn't do nothing, Elwayne." I put my arms around him.

He kissed me soft, then hungry, then soft again, like I'd always imagined boys kissed girls. His gentleness melted through me.

I sat down on the back step and listened to him walk away, loving even that about him. It took me a few minutes to notice the little noises in the woods again, sounds I told myself were nothing but birds. It took a few seconds more to realize that wasn't no bird when

Orris separated his shadow from a tree and moved across the splash of pale light coming from our back window.

Edging to my feet, I groped behind me for the door handle, hoping he couldn't tell I was still outside, but, of course, he could.

"Hey, Pert," he said.

Jobe had better be home. Truly and Papa weren't on their way home yet; I could still hear Pansy's joyful revival music.

I turned and grabbed for the handle. Missed.

Orris leaped and got me. He smashed me against the house.

"I know what you been doing with that ol' boy." Orris's voice grated.

He tightened his grip and I struggled. He pushed me against the wall and my head bumped hard. I wailed. He slapped my mouth.

The back door opened, and Jobe hollered, "Orris, what you think you're doing?" He jumped on Orris, yanked him off me. Orris broke free and ran for the forest.

"Now you've done it," I screamed after him. "I'm telling Lorelei. *Lorelei!*"

I sat down at the table. I was dizzy and sick at my stomach. Jobe guided me into the kitchen. Jobe had just painted the inside of the back door green, and the heavy smell of it made me even sicker.

Jobe knelt beside my chair and searched my face. "Pert, what in the world was going on?"

"You know Orris," I said, and tears choked me.

"Tell me what happened." His cheeks were thinner and more sunken than usual. This was Jobe mad, really mad.

"He's been after me."

Jobe jumped up. "I'm going to kill him."

"Don't leave me here alone," I begged.

He came back and sat down. "I'll kill him," he said, his teeth gritted together. "When Papa gets home . . ."

But I said, "No, Jobe, we aren't going to tell Papa. I'm going to tell Lorelei."

"This is for Papa and me to take care of."

"What about Mama?" I said. "You and Papa can't do nothing; she'd die. Lorelei's the only one."

Jobe frowned. "What if she don't believe you?"

"Maybe I won't tell her about me," I said. "I could tell her Orris is sleeping with Gloria."

Jobe sat back in his chair, his eyes empty of hope. "She's overlooked that kind of stuff for years."

"Maybe she won't overlook it if I tell her that he's sleeping with Gloria and everybody in Lexieville knows it."

Jobe looked at me, thought a minute. His eyes didn't change. "Deep down, she probably knows that, too."

But I couldn't give up; there had to be hope somewhere.

Early the next morning before Papa and Jobe got up for work, I went creeping to Lorelei.

I found her out by her chicken coop.

"Morning, Lorelei," I said, real quiet in case Orris was home, though I knew he'd never be awake this early.

"Morning, Pert," she said, and went over to her fence and stooped over a bag of chicken feed. "What's got you up so early of a morning? Want to help me with my chores?" She laughed.

"Why don't Orris come on out and help?" I said.

That got her. Everybody knew he lifted no fingers around there. She dug down into the feed and poured a scoopful into her bucket.

"Well, now, Pert, your uncle seems to be otherwise occupied this morning." She hefted the bucket, her face holier than ever, and turned to me. "What you doing out here, upsetting my chickens?"

"Lorelei," I said, and my heart shook loose. What if my words made no difference to her, after all? "I have to talk to you." I swallowed and breathed deep.

She stuck her hand down in the feed and broadcast

a fistful into the chicken yard, working like I wasn't there, like I hadn't said a word.

"I just thought, us being such close family friends and all, I ought to tell you. You ought to know."

She kept her face turned away from me. Would she listen? Would she care if I told her something she already knew?

Lorelei scooped into the bucket again; she watched the feed spill through her fingers. "Know what?"

"Lorelei, I just thought you should know."

She frowned.

I tried to make my mouth say Gloria's name, but I could see it wouldn't make any difference. I tried again, but instead I blurted, "It's Orris, Lorelei. He's been after me. Jobe stopped him last night and said if you don't do something about Orris, he will."

Lorelei's face went slack. She grabbed into the feed bucket, turned away from me, threw feed over the fence.

I had nothing else to say. I caught my lip between my teeth and waited.

She put her bucket down just so by the fence, her back to me. For a second, I wanted to reach for her. But I just stood there as she went on into the house, closed and latched the screen, then shut the wooden door and clicked its bolt into place.

⇒ Pert ⇐

Late September now and school back in session, here Raynell sat, at it again today. I looked around the lunch-room hoping to see Elwayne slide his long self toward us, but all I caught were the Sardis High School Fighting Swamp Cats banners, old "Just Say No!" posters, "Vote Todd Beck for Student Council President" signs, and the usual sideways looks Brittany Lee Hathaway and her friends from town gave us.

"Why'd Lorelei have to go and kick Orris out?" Raynell said for about the fifth time. Raynell whined morning, noon, and night about the fact that Lorelei kicked Orris out and that Gloria, Raynell's own mama, had taken him in. And I was the one who had to hear about it.

I didn't answer. If it weren't for Raynell bringing him up, I'd never waste a passing thought on Orris anymore.

I put my chin in my hand and sighed, hoping she'd see this was a boring subject.

She stopped and glanced down at her lunch tray, which she'd managed to empty like she did every day and still stay the skinniest girl alive. It hit me then that she wouldn't be much of a match to Orris if he ever decided to pick on her.

"Raynell," I said, the blood rushing in my ears. "Orris. He hasn't been trying anything with you, has he?"

She just sat there.

"I mean, Gloria's keeping a watch on him, isn't she?"

Raynell narrowed her eyes. "I guess if he messed with any of us, Mama'd about kill him. He knows that." Raynell stood, picked up her tray, and headed for the garbage line.

A bunch of laughter went up at Brittany Lee's table just about the time Raynell passed by. Brittany Lee pulled her hair down across the front of her face, hung her head, and pretended to be carrying a lunch tray. She was good at it — looked just like Raynell. Raynell didn't see a thing, but she heard the giggles and bowed even farther over her tray, her hair like curtains closing her in. Brittany Lee Hathaway glanced my way, saw I'd seen, and quit right quick.

It struck me like a fist in my chest. I tried to stare her down, but she just talked and laughed with the ones around her, acting like she'd never done anything and, for sure, hadn't ever caught my eye.

With nothing left of my lunch except a pile of fake mashed potatoes and pepper-flecked gravy I couldn't abide, I stood, scooted my chair in, and carried my tray slow and steady around behind Brittany Lee. I got a few quick looks from the girls across from her, which made her turn around and look at me.

Before she could turn back, I stumbled and — what do you know — I dumped my tray on her.

All her friends squealed.

I recovered my footing and said, "Oops, I'm so sorry."

She didn't accept my apology, only looked at me, her navy blue eyes so wide the white showed all the way round.

Her milk ran in a puddle across the table. BLH's friends all gave her napkins or dabbed at the front of her navy blue initial sweater, where all the potatoes and gravy had splashed and now slid clump by clump into her lap.

I was sorry, all right. Sorry I hadn't got her right square between those eyes.

It shouldn't have surprised me to get a note in my last-period class calling me down to the office after school, but it did.

Mr. Banes shoved his folded-up shirtsleeves higher, shuffled some papers around on his desk, pointed to the empty orange plastic chairs in front of his desk, and said, "Sit down." I sat. No Brittany Lee.

"Did you spill your tray on Brittany Lee today at lunch?"

I nodded.

His eyebrows drew together. "On purpose?"

My mouth went dry. "I stumbled and dropped my tray."

"Brittany Lee said you did it on purpose." He looked at me and waited.

"I told her I was sorry, but I guess she didn't hear me, what with all the commotion." I tried to look sincere and hoped that'd be enough to convince him. "Where is she? I'll tell her again."

"She's gone home. She had to catch her bus."

Hey, I had to catch my bus, too. Her house might be farther than mine, but she'd never have to walk it like I would. She could call anybody in school and they'd run in, elbowing each other out of the way just for the privilege of driving her home.

Mr. Banes pointed his pencil at me. "You'd better not let anything like this happen again, Pertrisha Lexie."

I nodded like I agreed.

Mr. Banes stood up. "You can go now."

I hurried out toward the bus line, but I'd already missed mine. The few cars still parked belonged to nobody who went my way. I started out, already tired, crossed the road, passed the quick-stop store, and turned onto the dirt road toward Lexieville. The trees, some already dried brown, had lost a few leaves, but most still held color: bright orange, red, yellow against the deep green pines and the shining blue sky. Not such a bad day for a walk.

I'd done okay with Mr. Banes. At least the truth was I really and truly didn't aim to drop my food on her sweater. Course I couldn't go ahead and mention I'd aimed at her big mouth, which she couldn't seem to keep shut.

Still, it was funny. I laughed. Right then, I didn't care if all of Sardis and Vernal, too, found out I got Brittany Lee Hathaway with the mashed potatoes and did it on purpose.

Here I was, one minute walking along happy and laughing my head off, the next minute looking at Orris standing in the road up ahead. I stopped dead.

He ran at me. Fear in my heart, I raced back down through the ruts toward Sardis. I didn't have a pencil on me, no hairpins, no nothing, just my running feet.

I heard him right behind me, gaining on me. He

almost caught hold of my shirt. I reached up and grabbed for a dangling tree limb to fight with.

Orris pounded on my back with both fists.

I lost my breath, fell forward. My hands scraped down along the limb's rough bark. My palms burned and my back felt about to cave in, but soon as I hit the ground I scrambled back up, gasped, tried to breathe again. But Orris tackled me. I hit the ground hard, and he knelt over me, pounding my stomach, my chest, my face.

"You bitch, you don't know nothing, you ain't nothing," he whined. "You ain't nothing."

I tried to cover my face with my arms. He hurt me so bad. I cried, and yelled, "Stop. Please, Orris, stop," and he did.

He stuck his face up close to mine. "I'm going to shut your big mouth," he whispered in his alcohol breath.

Orris shoved his fist in my face. Then he punched my throat, and I couldn't make any more sound. I lost all energy to move, just tasted blood.

He said in a sobby voice, "That'll teach you. That'll teach you."

Stop, stop. Please, God, make him stop.

But he kept on until everything in me felt broken.

Please.

Why had I told Lorelei? Why hadn't I just let him do what he wanted?

Orris crammed a handful of dirt, sticks, and bits of dried leaves into my mouth. He pressed down, mashed my nose. Dirt mixed with my breath.

Why hadn't I just pretended he was Elwayne, pulled his face to mine, put his hand on my belly? *I love you. Don't kill me.*

Underneath everything, under the screech and hum, beyond the swirled red and dark behind my eyes, a rattle, an engine.

Our truck coming down the road.

Papa. Jobe.

I screamed, but no sound, no air, only dust, filled my throat.

Papa yelled.

Jobe bellowed, "Orris."

Orris's fist slammed down on my head. Then just black and noise and nothing.

➤ Jobe ➤

Me and Papa seen her and Orris running toward us a ways down the road, almost couldn't tell who it was, but we both knew, said, "Pert," and Papa stepped on it about the time they turned and ran into the trees.

We were right there. I always wondered how he could've done so much damage so fast.

Papa jumped out the truck, nearly before it'd come to a stop good, and ran into the woods. Papa, who'd never raised his hands against a soul, pounded Orris upside the head. Orris ran. Papa fell right down to the ground, crying at her, "Pert, Pert," his voice all painful and thick.

I ran after Orris. We crashed through the leaves, deeper and deeper, my heart burning up. Never before had I felt such hate-fire. I would've been ready to kill anybody'd hurt Pert, but him being Orris only made it worse. My heart bursting inside me, I chased him down. I would be a devil from hell if it took that to catch him.

I yelled and tackled him, knocked his wind out, and I had him. I got him around the throat and squeezed. He landed a fist on my face a couple of times, so I stopped choking him and beat his face to blood.

His flesh caved in and his bones broke. I filled my fingers with his bloody, feathery hair. I stood over him, sweat running into my eyes, and kicked up and down his whole body, stomped him with my boots, until he neither fought nor moved.

His blood pooled in the dirt and clotted on his face. I fell down panting beside him. I gnashed my teeth, thought I would die, too. And I didn't care.

Numb, I waited. But Death didn't come for me. As dusk fell, I came to my senses and sat up.

I hid Orris under a pile of leaves and sticks, then went deeper into the woods, circled around, and ended up on a path I knew behind our house. At the creek, I washed the blood away, watched it darken the water then disappear. But I knew I'd see his blood on my hands forever.

That devil from hell had helped me catch Orris, but now it had taken up residence inside me. That devil had killed Orris. That devil was me.

❧ Pert ❧

Papa gathered me in his arms, picked me up, and ran with me. I had to think: *Open your mouth. Cough. Spit out dirt. Breathe.*

Papa cried, "Pert, Pert, Pert." His voice cracked and echoed around the forest.

But I didn't cry.

Quiet on the road — it'd never been so calm — except for this little breeze that rustled the old brown leaves on a low branch. That breeze blew on my face all the way home.

Papa pulled me from the truck. But it hurt.

My bed. Screams.

Truly. Her hands on me. Pain, and her sobs. I tried to see her. Just dark.

Papa's voice. Mama and Papa in the kitchen.

Her hands. Water, cool in my mouth. My body afire, then softness, soothing darkness. Darkness.

All night he came to me, his face purple, his eyes bulging. He killed me and killed me. Orris stood over me, then I stood beside him. Together we looked at my dead body, my throat marked with his handprints, my face blue. Now we were children, sitting in the dirt, crawling around and pushing little toy cars, scooping out roads with large pieces of bark. For a while it was Jobe and me building a city around that body, digging a river under its bent knee, spreading the hair out for a lake, pretending the cupped hands were our houses. Jobe laughed his little-boy laugh, and I looked over at him. But it was Orris now, a laughing boy. He pushed his toy car to my right hand. He walked his fingers across the dirt, onto my hand, across my blue-veined wrist, up my arm. Dodging bruises, the fingers hopped onto my chin, then nose, then forehead, and dove into the lake water. His fingers disappeared into my hair.

I slept all the next day, but Jobe came and roused me sometime in there. He said, "Orris is gone. He ain't going to bother you no more. Just get well."

The words echoed around in my head, and I slept again. A large house, long and narrow. I walked from room to room, deeper and deeper. People in each room pointed to the next, whispered, "Orris is gone." Flooded rooms, no furniture, windows with sunshine beyond, water deeper in each room until it came up to my waist. The whispers there said, "Jobe is gone. Gone." A stop sign, red and huge, posted on the door to the last room made me stop, look in that room and out through its window, angry blue-gray sea to the horizon, Jobe out there somewhere.

The doctor Mrs. Turnbull sent touched me, seared my body, said, "No broken bones."

Papa's hand tilted my head forward and Mama's fingers pried my mouth open. "You got to take it, doctor said," she whispered, and Papa said, "Please, Pert." I opened my mouth.

I had to leave those dream rooms, turn around at that sign, stop searching the stormy sea for Jobe.

I slept without dreams for a long time after that.

❧ Jobe ❧

Raynell took me by the hand the day after we brought Pert in broken and bloody. I clutched hold of her and thought I'd never be able to let go. She led me to the mission building and we sat on its back steps as the earth creaked on over into night. I cried till my eyes had no more tears, and she patted on my back like I was just a baby. I knew because of what I'd done it wouldn't never be the same with Raynell again, but that night I couldn't get up and leave. Not till she said she'd best get on home.

I walked her to her house, then the night fell, like broken pieces, around me. I went back down to the mission, pulled by the peace I'd felt with Raynell there. The back door to the mission stood open, and I walked in. Like I already knew what my fate had to be. I walked right in, and there was Reverend Blankenship, down on his knees, sweating and moving his lips with no sound, his elbows propped on the back of a chair.

He unfolded himself and came over to stand before me.

From a crate near the heater came a rustling. I shivered.

"Brother Jobe, why are you here?"

"I come seeking my salvation," I whispered.

Cusper Blankenship put his hand on my shoulder and nodded. "I've been praying for you," he murmured, and guided me toward the crate.

He opened the crate and I stared into the pile of straw where the rattlesnake lay curled around itself, looped and twisted. He reached into the crate and brought that shining snake into the light. I saw my only path and held out my hands to accept it.

❧ Truly ❧

Nearly every day I go looking for Orris. Sometimes Raynell sees me walking and brings me home. Pert's always asleep on her cot. Raynell says she'll be hungry, they all will be hungry, and helps me decide what to cook, rinses the dried beans, puts on the rice, brushes my hair before Jobe and John get home.

Every night I wake myself crying, tears on my face, and I hear Pert over there breathing. I mustn't fall asleep. If I do she might stop. I sit up and stare into the dark around her cot. I try to pray, but all I can say is, "Why?"

As Reverend Cusper says and I know, we are weak and heavy-laden, we are sinking deep in sin, watching for the thief in the night, washed in the blood, sinking to rise no more.

≈ Pert ≈

When Elwayne brought me my schoolwork, I wouldn't let him see me. I no longer looked at my face, either, all swollen tight. I ran my fingers over my cheeks, barely touched the skin, so tender; ran them over bumps and scratches, ran them over my puffy eyes, soft and sore. I tried to do the homework, but all the *O*'s and zeroes on the pages looked like they wanted to spell out *Orris,* so I mostly slept.

Days later, when I woke up and couldn't sleep anymore, I remembered things: a picnic on the big flat rock. Sunshine and early spring. Truly and Jobe and Papa and me. Papa put his arms around Truly, whispered in her ear. She put back her head and laughed at me watching them. Jobe and I had wildflowers in our hands, stained palms. I took mine to Truly, stood on tiptoe to reach that high rock, held them up.

And in town. The Wal-Mart, aisles and aisles of toys, some dollar bills in my hand. Papa watched us sort through the hanging packages to find something that matched the money. Papa and Truly rode back home in the truck cab, Jobe, Orris, and me in the back.

Orris'd bought a package of caramel corn, and we passed it back and forth. Some of the kernels got snatched up by the wind and Orris tried to grab them back. But they blew away and he stuck his tongue out and crossed his eyes. Jobe and I laughed; nearly choked on that caramel corn, we laughed so hard.

That memory Orris felt like a different person. Someone who'd gone long ago. Not the real Orris.

Nothing could make me see the sense in anything about Orris Lexie now. Nothing about this life made sense anymore. Nothing.

Jobe brought me Coca-Colas and things from the store. He sat beside me in the evening and held my hand. Sometimes he read to me from the newspaper. Sometimes the newspaper shook as he read all about Little Rock, the shootings and stabbings, the comics, our horoscopes. We didn't talk because all there was to say was about Orris, and neither of us could talk about him anymore. No one knew where Orris was now, but I hoped he was sick as I was somewhere, sick and hurt, and would never bother me again. Jobe's hands were rough and scabby, and he had a greenish bruise or two near his eyes. Orris had put up a fight, I guess.

One evening after a couple of weeks had passed and I still wasn't much better, Reverend Cusper Blankenship and his wife, Pansy, came by for a visit. Pansy handed Truly a big black enamel pot. The smell of chicken and celery made my stomach roll. Truly smiled at me, said, "Look here what Pansy has brought," and went on through to the kitchen.

The Blankenships, Papa, and Jobe gathered around me and whispered together, like I couldn't hear.

"How is the poor little thing?" Pansy said, and looked at Papa like he was a poor little thing.

He glanced down at me. Cusper clasped Jobe up in a hug, said, "Have faith, Brother Jobe," and patted his back till Jobe shook like a loose-limbed doll.

Truly came back from the kitchen and fell in there between Papa and Jobe. Cusper placed his right hand on my head, and Pansy, on the other side of me, laid her left hand beside his. They all bowed their heads, except for Cusper, who looked up into the rafters and called on the name of the Lord.

"Dear Lord," he said in his preacher's voice, "we beseech Your heavenly presence to take notice on us, poor sinners, to forgive and heal this one, a lamb of Your flock, snared by wolves and wounded in body and spirit. . . ."

The others whispered, "Amen," and, "Yes, Lord," around the circle. But I lost interest right off, when he brought up forgiveness. What did he ask God to forgive *me* for? It was Orris should be worried about that. No matter what, forgiveness from me wasn't something Orris'd ever see. He could beg and plead. He could be good to me all the days of his life and I'd still never forgive.

Cusper's praying went on and on for maybe an hour. His voice rose and fell. His and his wife's hands got warmer on my head. Sniffles and more prayer words came from the others. Twilight grayed the windows, and soon it grew darker inside than out. In the soft buzz and murmur of their voices, their hands heavy, my eyes closed and I slept.

After that Jobe took less time to read to me, and more time just to hold my hand and sit. Looked like he prayed, but I guess he was just tired. He started taking turns with Papa walking Truly to church so Papa could stay and sit with me.

One morning after Papa and Jobe left for work, Truly woke me. She smoothed my hair and asked, "Are you hungry?"

I shook my head no.

After a while, she said, "This you ought to know, Pert." She cleared her throat, then said, "Your papa and Jobe chased Orris off that day. They think he believes he's killed you, so I expect he will stay away from Lexieville now. You rest and get well and don't worry no more."

I couldn't tell her that was all I was now — worried I'd never get well and away from here, never get away from Orris. "I'm not worried," I said.

"But you seem unsettled in your sleep," she said, and I noticed how her eyes had purplish circles under them. "Why don't you just try not to think about it anymore?"

I nodded and sank back on my pillow. My mama got up and went over and stood by the kitchen door. She whispered, "I'm sorry, Pert." I pretended to sleep.

She went on into the kitchen. The first tears I'd cried since Orris got me stung my eyes. I opened my mouth and made a sound I'd never heard myself or anyone else make before. I shut my mouth, but not before a tear rolled in. Salt. And I remembered: blood from my cut-up lips, the way it dried in the wind blowing through the truck window, the way it tightened the skin around my mouth.

That was when I thought I would never get well.

Truly

My head hurts behind my eyes. Under my eyelids my eyes feel so huge and dry that I fear they will not open and I will be trapped here in this red world filled with pain.

And Pert's face. I see her face, bruised, eyes blue-black and puffed up. She lies so still, her eyes swollen so tight no tear could ever squeeze out. I know how it is to die but keep on living, keep on with your heart beating inside your ears, pounding your head at night. Heart like a creature all its own, banging against your ribs, keeping you awake, making you remember.

I know Orris is out there somewhere too afeared to come, too ashamed. I whisper, "Orris, I'm cooking up a batch of chicken and dumplin's for my dinner. Come eat with me and I promise, ever'thing will be all right."

Ice cold, he is, and won't come running to Truly for help. Poor little brother.

"Just come quiet and come early, before they get home. Can't let no one hear you. Come in and eat, but don't talk in my kitchen, little brother."

I go ahead and set out the stew pot and bowl on the table, fill the pot half full with water from the bucket, start up our butane cookstove, thankful the tank is full again, and set the water on to boil.

I grab my butcher knife, go out into the cooling afternoon sun to the chicken coop. Then I grab me up a hen by her neck and wring it.

At the edge of the trees I commence plucking and cutting.

I slice off the feet, muscles still jerking, then open it up, reach my hand in, and rake out the warm, beating innards, throw them all in a pile. The day's gone cool enough now to see the steam rise up into the air like a ghost. I watch it ease away through the ragged black weeds, then I stick the butcher knife through the hen's neck and carry it out at arm's reach, blood draining onto the dry grass, muscles white with pink and bluish tints, fat, yellow-globbed, ready to make Orris some mighty fine dumplings.

Inside my kitchen, cloudy from the boiling vapor, I slide the chicken off the knife down through the *steam, where it disappears in a splash that sizzles on the burner. I go to work with the flour, mixing up the dumplings in the bowl while the simmering broth smells like comfort to me. Salt. A little baking powder. From under the kitchen sink, I take the box of that rat poison John brought home last spring. Never did make a bit of difference to those mice.*

I open the box, shake in a little, enough I figure, but not so much to carry too heavy a taste.

I lay my head over on the table and wait for the chicken to cook tender enough to add the dough. Fat bubbly dumplings puff up across the broth, and it smells good. I lower the heat and put on the lid, put away the dry ingredients, wash up my dumpling bowl and spoon, dust off the table.

The broth simmers under the lid, the only sound in my house until the box underneath Pert's cot drags across the wood floor, out then back. The cot springs creak. In the quiet, I wait, and it's only my heart in my ears I hear and the dumplings boiling. A cough. It's Pert; Pert's in there. At the doorway I peek in, afraid of her bruises. She sits there, leaned back against the wall with her eyes closed.

She opens her eyes, says to me, "Hi, Mama," where she usually only calls me Truly, and I know it for a miracle, like Cusper has been promising over and over from the first day to this. I rejoice and my feet take me to her. My hands reach out and shake as I touch her arm, her cheek. Warm, but my hands are cold.

I stroke her hair and she lifts her face up to me, looks at me with eyes as blue and sad as Orris's always were. I gaze at my girl and catch a glimpse of the small spot in her neck beating a pulse, see her chest rise with her breath, hear its whisper in and out her open mouth. She's watching my face, close, like what she sees there means something more than just my features. She looks at me all full of sorrow for a moment before she drops her head on my shoulder and puts her arms, heavy, around me. She clings to me like a baby and sobs.

I can't breathe. I pat her arm and try to stand up. "Time for us to rest now."

I manage to help her lie down and cover her with her quilt, trying not to see that devil confusion growing in her eyes.

"Stretch out and rest for a while. You'll feel better afterward," *I say. She turns her head away from me and curls up under her covers.*

I can hardly drag myself over to climb into my own bed and pull my quilt up over my head.

⇒ Pert ⇐

I woke up to the steamy smell of chicken broth. I yawned, sat up and got a sweatshirt from the box under my cot, put it on, then leaned my head back against the newspapered wall, and closed my eyes.

Truly came in. I opened my eyes, and she came closer. She touched my face, tracing my bruises. For a few minutes, it seemed like it used to be, like when I was little. She knew I belonged to her.

I reached out, and she let me hold on to her. Orris's cold hands around my heart let go a little. I cried and held tighter, wishing she'd rock me, sing, "Hush-a-bye, don't you cry," in her thin, high voice. I tried to make my ears hear it, but she pulled away.

"Lie down," she said. "We'll rest now."

His hands squeezed again.

I should've known. Orris's sister couldn't be my mother again.

I stared at the foggy front window, made my mind just as blank and gray. I listened to Truly whimper in her sleep, to the chicken broth boiling in the kitchen. No other sounds until Jobe came in.

"I didn't hear the truck," I whispered. I stretched and I hurt all over. "Where's Papa?"

Jobe glanced at Truly and whispered back, "He wanted to stop for a few groceries, and I wanted to come home. Mrs. Turnbull gave me a ride on her way to Gloria's. Maybe I'll go visit Raynell after a while." He halfway grinned.

He acted so comfortable about Raynell by now I couldn't even tease him anymore, so I just said, "Truly has something cooking already. You may as well go ahead."

Jobe went into the kitchen, clinked the lid against the pot, and came to the door. "Chicken and dumplin's. Want some?"

"Not now. I'll get some later."

Pretty soon I could hear his fork clicking against his plate. I got hungry. I swung my legs off the cot but caught my heel in the box I hadn't quite pushed all the way back under. It tipped. The racket roused Truly.

She rolled over toward me and pulled the cover off her head. "What you doing, Pert? You feeling all right?" she asked, her voice sleepy.

"I'm feeling pretty good. I got a nice nap," I lied, though I didn't believe she really cared. "I'm just going in to eat supper with Jobe."

Truly sat up so tall, it was like she had a string attached from the top of her head to the rafters. Her face went pale. Then that string pulled her straight up to stand on the bed. She covered her face with shaky fingers. Her wild eyes looked back at me, around the room, stopped at the kitchen door. Truly leaped off the bed and ran across the gray-and-dusty-rose floorboards into the kitchen.

"Stop, Jobe!" she screamed, and tore the fork from his hand. "That's Orris's supper," she hissed.

Jobe stared at the fork, his mouth open.

She grabbed his plate, dumped it into the stew pot, and yelled, "Don't eat Orris's dumplin's."

Jobe shut his mouth, looked about to cry, and chewed the mouthful he'd already taken.

But Truly, her face red and swollen, rushed at him, slapped him on the back, put her palm to his mouth. "Spit it out," she ordered.

He opened his mouth and let the dumpling dribble out into her hand. Truly opened the door and flung the handful out far as she could. She wiped her wet hand along the side of her dress. She looked at Jobe, her eyes huge and sad. "Those dumplin's were for Orris, not you."

She grabbed the boiling pot by its hot metal handles with her bare hands and lifted it off the burner.

"That's hot!" Jobe jumped up to stop her.

"Get back," she yelled. The broth sloshed down her front. Through the rising steam, tears on her face, she said again, "It's for Orris." She stumbled outside.

I stood at the door, unable to move for a minute. Truly walked stiff-legged with the strain of the heavy pot; the greasy broth soaked her dress, ran down her legs onto her bare feet.

I went after her. "Stop, Mama, you're burning yourself."

At the trees she set the pot down and tipped it over. Chicken and dumplings spilled out across the pine needles. Broth pooled round her feet. I wanted to bring her in and wash her off with a cool cloth. I reached toward her to pull her back. Jobe ran past me.

Halfway to the outhouse he stopped, doubled over, and vomited.

Still bent over, he unbuckled his belt and stumbled to the door. The spring at the top stretched, rang one rusty note. He went in, and the door slammed shut behind him. Truly knelt down in the broth and shoved her mouth full of the mess she'd spilled on the ground.

I reached her, and the hot broth stung through my socks. I pulled her hands away from her gaping mouth, away from her face smeared with damp, floury dough.

"Stand up," I said. I tried to pull her up, but she tilted sideways, slid off her knees, and sat flat on the ground.

Truly's face changed from pink to a color no darker than the dough around her mouth. "I poisoned Orris," she said.

Dark whirled around inside me. I grasped her wrists and pulled. Her arms straightened out toward me, and she fell over. She opened her mouth, tried to throw up. Nothing. She lay her cheek on the pine needles as if they were the softest of pillows and she ready for sleep.

I pulled her again, tried to make her sit up. Her hand swatted my face; it made me cry, just like a slap, then made me mad. I fought her flailing arms and convulsing body to drag her across the earth, out of the hot broth.

Her tremors stopped. Fear ran up and down my back. I cried at her, and tears rolled into my mouth. I grabbed her hands and held them, but she moved her fingers inside my hands, tried to get loose.

She convulsed again, harder than before, thrashing so much I couldn't hold her. Her teeth gnashed her tongue. Blood spattered my hands. Her head tossed side to side.

She stiffened, then she went limp and gray. Her eyes rolled up under their lids, the skin around her eyes stained blue. No breath at all, not even my own. In the silence, my ears rang.

The air stirred, brushing my arm as if Truly had reached for me before her soul lifted away through the trees. The bare branches trembled. I shook all over, shook so bad my teeth rattled together.

Jobe groaned. I turned.

The world blazed bright, brittle-edged and too sharp in focus, then grew dull. Jobe sat propped up against the corner of the outhouse, his face only a shade lighter than the boards.

"Jobe." I ran toward him as if in a dream, pushing through the thick air, parting it before me like wet sheets hung out to dry. "Jobe, Jobe, Jobe, Jobe, Jobe, Jobe!" I screamed, and the echoes ran through me as I touched his hot face.

He reached up and squeezed my wrists, tried to pull my hands away. But I held him and searched his eyes, tried to call him back. He released my hands and turned his face from me. He panted, shallow and fast.

Papa's truck rattled up out front.

Low in his throat, Jobe rasped out, "Get Papa."

Papa slammed his door and whistled a few notes.

I ran around the house. Dizzy, I stopped for a second, bent over, tried to make my voice work. I managed to call out, "Papa," straightened up, and called again. "Papa, Papa." I reached him and grabbed on to him. "Help us, Papa, help us."

Papa steadied us both and looked at me deep. His face changed. His eyes squeezed shut and his teeth ground together — almost like he already knew — and he left me behind. He ran faster than I'd ever seen him go. And I knew he had run just as fast for me that day in the woods.

Papa fell down beside Jobe, put his hands all over Jobe's face, said, "He's too hot," and tugged on Jobe's shirt, got it off him. Jobe was trembling.

I squatted down, covered my face with my hands. I could hardly say it. "Papa, it's not just Jobe. It's Mama, too. It was poison, Papa. They ate poison."

Papa looked up, and all the lines on his forehead and around his eyes deepened. I pointed at that spot by the woods where the cooking pot lay, where nothing moved, not a leaf nor a limb, not a finger nor a curl of hair.

Papa tried to stand. He tipped over, caught himself with one hand, then moaned and pushed away from the earth.

He dropped to his knees beside Truly and sobbed, heavy and loud. Our hearts broke together, and I wanted to fall down beside him and give in to the pain.

Instead, I ran. I tore through the trees and across my old clearing. I crashed through the underbrush, screamed, "Lorelei," again and again.

SPRING COUNTY WELFARE DEPARTMENT
HOME VISIT FORM

SOCIAL WORKER: Alice Turnbull   # SC 7

CLIENT: John Lexie family

ADDRESS: Lexieville Rd. (2nd house on left)

PURPOSE: Determine family and individual needs following Truly Lexie's death at age 35.

FINDINGS: Household in disarray. John in shock, almost unable to function. Jobe treated and released after 48 hours of hospitalization for ingestion of a poisonous substance. In my inspection of the dwelling I came across a box of RodentOut! in the cupboard next to the flour and baking soda. When questioned, Pertrisha said it was usually kept under the kitchen sink, but suggested that her mother may have introduced it into the dumplings by mistake (the dumplings being the vehicle for the poison in both the case of her mother and her brother), stating that her mother had been distracted and upset lately.

RECOMMENDATIONS:

- *John (37):* Immediate medical attention. Complete checkup and medication for anxiety and to help him cope with grief. To be followed by individual psychological counseling as needed, in addition to regular meetings with me.
- *Jobe (18):* Follow-up medical care and regular sessions with me.
- *Pertrisha (17):* Sessions with me as needed to keep her on track with her post–high school plans once her recuperation period is over.

FOLLOW-UP: Check in with them twice weekly over the next two weeks, then return to monthly home visits in approximately six weeks.

⇜ Pert ⇝

I sat next to Papa in the front pew of the First Send-the-Light Gospel church as the funeral-home people rolled in my mama's gray metal casket covered with the spray of white carnations and yellow bows Papa had picked out special. He'd said the ribbons couldn't be nothing but yellow, like the daffodils Mama watched for every spring. Mama used to say they meant no winter would last forever.

Pansy and the choir started in on "Whispering Hope," Lorelei's heavy soprano carrying the tune. The sound came to me through thick curtains of air, like I couldn't get up and move through if I needed to. If I was thankful for anything, it was that I could sit here and not have to move anything but my eyes.

In a folding chair behind the pulpit, Jobe sat wearing his newest jeans, a blue-jean jacket, a white shirt, and a skinny black tie. Papa had located his old black suit in a box up in the rafters. Funerals were not what we Lexies were prepared for. I wasn't any different, except that Mrs. Turnbull'd found me somebody's old navy pleated-skirt dress with a big square collar edged in crocheted beige lace.

A man from the funeral home walked up to Papa and shook his hand. He whispered, "I'll be opening the casket now, if that's okay."

Papa's eyes focused on the man's hand grasping his.

That man none of us knew went over to the casket and lifted the lid. I braced myself. I hadn't seen her yet. She lay on a shiny white pillow, her hair curled like from a beauty shop. Somebody had given her a facial, pink on her cheeks and lipstick, neither of which I'd ever seen her wear, even for Papa. There came a squeezing in the middle of my chest, and I didn't know if it might be worse or better that she looked not a bit like herself. Papa sobbed beside me, and I put my arms around him. I didn't have a hand to wipe my own tears, so I just let them fall on his musty old suit coat.

Cusper stood up, cleared his throat, read a scripture about ashes and dust, said how we'd come here to celebrate the life of our late sister, Truly Lexie, and read her obituary like it came straight out of the newspaper.

"A homemaker and lifelong resident of Lexieville, Truly Amelia Lexie is survived by her husband, John, son, Jobe, daughter, Pertrisha, and brother, Orris Lexie, all of Spring County, Arkansas." At the mention of Orris, Jobe looked at me and I looked at him. "Truly was a fine Christian woman and will be grievously missed by her many friends in this community and by her family."

Cusper sat down, and I couldn't help but think that didn't sound like much of a celebration to me. Now it was Jobe's turn. He got up and rocked from foot to foot and clasped his hands together in front of him before he could manage to take a step toward the pulpit.

"Truly Amelia Lexie, my mother, had a hard life growing up here in Lexieville. She never had much time for school and study, things like that, and lately she hasn't been all that well, but she did the best she knew how, raised up me and my sister, Pert, fed us, took care of us when we were sick. She made us up quilts from the clothes we outgrew, was a fine woman and helpmate to our daddy, a good friend to people around here, took an interest in this church mission and was a good sister, too."

Sister. Why'd he have to call up Orris's face to our minds again? Nobody here wanted to think about him.

Jobe looked at me, then up at the far corner of the room. "Truly Lexie wasn't one for fancy things, but liked a pretty flower more than just about anything."

That made me picture all the times when we were little and we picked a bunch of buttercups or black-eyed Susans and brought them in to her and she smiled and hugged and sang us some song I couldn't now remember, a country song or maybe a church song, something about flowers. Then while Jobe went on to quoting scripture about lilies of the field, I remembered how Orris used to sneak up behind Truly, tiptoeing, his hands behind his back full of scraggly wildflowers and a bottle to share.

Jobe was still quoting that verse "Don't worry about tomorrow," and I couldn't figure out how it fit in with today or Truly or any of us. All I did now was worry about tomorrow.

"'Each day,'" he went on, finishing the quote, "'has trouble enough of its own.'" Now *that* I understood. I nodded, and he appeared somehow satisfied, walked from the podium, and sat down, this time next to Raynell.

The choir sang "Crossing the Bar" and people passed by between us and the casket paying their respects. Elwayne was one of the last. I couldn't even look at him. When the congregation had filed out, Jobe joined us, and Cusper shook all our hands. We got up and moved against what felt like a great wind and stood looking down on Truly together. My knees wanted to bend and let me sink down on the floor, but I held tight to Jobe's wrist. Our mama's eyes looked glued shut, and her nose too narrow. Her makeup blurred up close. I backed up, and nobody stopped me. I sat down on the front pew. Papa's short hair looked odd, like he had tried to oil and comb it. Jobe's hair curled along his neck. Without his mother there, who would tell him it needed a cut? Who would do that now? Who would tell us the things a mother says?

Jobe put his arm around Papa, motioned to me, and led Papa down the aisle. I couldn't get up yet. I didn't want to sit and look at Truly, but I couldn't help it. What had she gone and done, what had she gone and done? Who would take care of Papa and Jobe if I left, too? The funeral man nodded to me and turned to let the lid down. A shadow closed over Mama's face before the lid hid it forever.

The funeral-home man placed the flowers on top of the casket, and the pallbearers came from their quiet places in the back to carry my mother away.

Now I knew I'd never be able to leave Lexieville.

⊱ Jobe ⊰

I helped Papa down the aisle and out of the church. Raynell stood waiting for us in the sunlight. At the hearse, I got Papa seated, and we waited for Pert and Mama. First came the casket all closed down and sealed, then Pert hurried out and climbed in beside Papa, her face pinched up and pale. She sat there, squeezing Papa's hand tight with her own and trying to catch her breath. But not crying. I broke down, and Raynell held my head to her shoulder. I wished then, with all my heart and soul — I wished, but I didn't know what for.

⇜ Pert ⇝

Truly hadn't done anything to keep Orris from hurting me, but somehow her being gone made me feel less safe in this world than before. I locked the doors when Papa and Jobe left and even moved chairs and boxes in front of them, though deep down I knew nothing I did would make me safe. No magic nor skill could ever stop Orris.

At night, Papa, all bowed down with his own sorrow, would sit with me a few minutes. He couldn't look at my bruises for long, and he wouldn't talk about Truly at all. He said things like, "You'll be back to your pretty little self again soon," and, "Go ahead and cry if you need to, honey."

I just said, "Tell me all about work today," and he told me Mrs. Turnbull asked them to paint down at the welfare department. He said she'd finally seen how bad her own hallway looked.

"Will it be that bright yellow again?"

"No, she wants smoke blue with mauve trim this time."

I wouldn't say anything, but I was sorry to see the yellow go, even old as it was. I wondered what other things had changed. Things might just as well change around me, because most everything'd changed inside. For sure, I had no more ideas about wooden cases or boundary fences. I'd never be brave again. I didn't even care anymore what Brittany Lee Hathaway did or said. But one thing I'd learned: what she said about Lexies was most likely true.

One night while Papa sat with me, I guess I fell asleep, because he patted my shoulder, said, "Listen, Pert, I got to say this about Orris."

My papa stopped for a minute, rubbed his eyes. Then he leaned forward and touched my forehead like he did when he checked me for fever. He said, "Jobe told me what he saw happen with you and Orris. You should've told me, Pert. I could've taken care of it."

I shook my head and told him, "I hope when Mrs. Turnbull and the sheriff catch up to him and he tries fighting" — my voice got louder — "they'll just kill him."

Papa held me close. "Don't you worry about him no

more. We won't let him hurt you. You just work on getting better."

But Papa couldn't stop the worry or the sickness inside. Orris would come back. Right that minute, he could be just outside our door.

A few days later, when Papa saw I wasn't getting better, he said, "We're going to take you to services tonight."

I didn't want to go anywhere, but especially not there, not where we'd gone to bury Truly. "I'm not going," I told him.

Papa said, "Come on, Pert, you might be surprised."

"No." I pulled my quilt over my head, but couldn't stop the vision of that casket lid closing down over Truly's face.

"Jobe," Papa called.

Jobe came in, tugged the cover off my face, said, "No arguments, Pert."

"Please, Papa."

He took my hands and pulled me up. "Your mama would want you to go."

I didn't have the energy to argue. It didn't really matter. I already knew nothing could help.

Papa and I walked in the front door of the mission together. But Jobe waved and went round toward the back. He must've gone to find Raynell or maybe even decided to skip it. I wouldn't blame him.

Tonight everything went along about as I'd expected; everybody acted like crazy was holy. Under the white-painted rafters, Pansy and Cusper worked as a team. She played loud or soft depending on what Cusper wanted the people in the pews to feel. Loud, and the congregation shouted, "Hallelujah, amen." Quiet, and they wiped their eyes. All along Papa kept checking on my reaction, and all along I ignored him, my stomach hollow with memories of Truly.

Toward the end, people got more and more worked up. They all stood to clap, sway, and sing — even Papa. Cusper kept on with his preaching, and picked up a wooden crate and set it on a table beside his pulpit. He set a second one beside it and opened their lids. Somebody'd chopped a cross into one, and the words *Jesus Saves* they'd carved a bit neater into the other.

Pansy played loud and fast, and the crowd clapped and sang and shouted. When Jobe appeared and stepped up to the pulpit, I grabbed Papa's arm and said, "What's happening?"

Cusper dug into the crates and brought out three live rattlesnakes. He showed them to the congregation.

"What's Jobe doing up there?" I asked, but Papa didn't seem to hear.

Cusper held the snakes out toward Jobe — the least one first, then the middle-sized one, then this great big one.

Jobe took the first two, one in each hand. He held them at arm's length, then Cusper draped the great big ugly one around Jobe's neck. I swear it had eyes just like Orris. I sat too scared to move. I couldn't speak, and I couldn't look away.

"Hallelujah," Cusper shouted.

Jobe focused his gaze on the ceiling fans while the big snake curved and slid down his chest and around under one arm. The snake's body followed in waves until its rattler flicked up beside Jobe's ear and its head reappeared over his shoulder. Jobe relaxed his grip on the other snakes, and they began a slow glide up his arms. The reptiles crawled up and around him like ropes looped round and round a captive. The ropes overlapped and tightened.

His eyes uplifted, his face alight, Jobe changed before me. When he looked back at the crowd, it was as if he were staring each and every one of us straight in the eye. The air around us boiling with reptiles, we all saw ourselves held captive by evil.

Pansy swung into "When the Roll Is Called up Yonder," and the people joined in singing about when time shall be no more. Papa's voice rose along with them.

Jobe turned his attention to the rattlers, starting with the least. He grabbed it behind the head. Its forked tongue flicked the air, and its body went limp. My brother, Jobe, brought it to his face and peered into its eyes. Cusper moved in, and Jobe handed that snake over. The same with the second one. That left only the big one with Orris's eyes.

Jobe turned his head and looked over his shoulder to where the big one's head rested. The snake turned its head and looked at me. There before me were good and evil, side by side.

Jobe frowned and inched his right hand up to his left shoulder, took hold of that scaly head and held its jaws shut. Its Orris eyes bugged out, and the rattles clattered and echoed through that white-walled room like hail on a roof.

Cusper held out a wooden crate, and Jobe threw Orris in there, slapped shut the lid, and hooked the latch.

Jobe's cheek shone pink. He looked like he'd seen an angel. Or maybe he'd become one. People clapped their hands, shouted for joy, and spilled into the aisles, arms raised and mouths open. Pansy grabbed Jobe and hugged him. He didn't hug her back or even move, so Pansy took his arm and slapped his palm on her head. She had her eyes closed now, her lips moving. Lorelei came up and flopped his other hand down on her own head.

Jobe stood there letting the whole bunch take turns standing under his hands. People waited in line, then passed Jobe's hands on to the next when Cusper tapped their shoulders to move on. They went back to their seats for Bibles, coats, and purses, then shuffled out the door murmuring, "Oh, Lordy, Lordy," "Praise Jesus," or "Bless him. Bless that boy, Jobe."

Papa went up to Jobe, but I stayed put. How could he have let Jobe do that? Jobe trembled with Papa's arms around him, both of them as far from me now as Truly was in death. Weak and sick, I sank back into the pew.

When I couldn't stand to watch them anymore, I looked away. Elwayne, over by a window under a dim light, sat watching me. I covered my face. I still hadn't seen myself in a mirror, but I knew my face'd be yellow-stained from old bruises. There was a bump that didn't go away on the bridge of my nose, and my whole nose felt tilted, off center.

I glanced at him again, and he was making his way over to me, his eyebrows high like he was surprised I saw him, but pleased. I'd missed him, and I hadn't noticed it until now.

I kept a hand over as much of my face as I could.

"You going forward?" he asked, and sat down beside me.

I laughed like what he said was a joke.

He shrugged. "I wondered, seeing it's Jobe." He took my hand away from my face and looked at my nose, my cheeks, my forehead.

I turned back toward Jobe. His pale skin lay tight on his cheekbones, and his nose looked thinner and longer.

Elwayne said, "I came by to visit you, but every time, they said to wait awhile."

He looked at me and whispered, "I went after Orris that night. I took the hunting rifle and went for him."

"Did you find him?" I whispered.

His eyes narrowed and he shook his head. "No, I never did. I followed some tracks all the way from the woods up to your back door. I guess they must have been Jobe's, going home."

I nodded. "He chased Orris away."

"I wanted to find him, Pert." He put his arm around my shoulder and pulled me over to lean on him, and I didn't care where we were or who saw. He felt good.

A thud from the pulpit made us look up. Jobe was sitting on the podium step, his hands over his face, his whole body shaking. His pants legs, too short anyway, had hiked up to show his white socks. Papa and the

Blankenships just stood there. Raynell squatted down beside Jobe and put her hand on his arm.

I stood up and said, "I'd better go see if Jobe's okay."

"Can I help?" Elwayne asked.

"Maybe you can walk Raynell home. I don't think Jobe will be able to."

Elwayne nodded. "I'll come see you tomorrow," he said, and slipped off the pew and went up to Raynell.

After Elwayne and Raynell left, Cusper and Papa helped Jobe stand. He leaned on them for a few steps. When he looked up and saw me, he left them and came over to me, his face all wet from tears.

"Pert, things is going to get better now," he said, like he was going to be a big shield between me and the whole world.

Jobe leaned on me, and my knees sank down. Jobe straightened right up and took his weight off me. Papa joined us and we walked down the aisle and out the door. We zipped up our jackets, but the cold crept out of the ground and up our legs. We stepped out into the dirt road between two dark walls of trees and followed a narrow strip of starry sky home.

We walked like that for a while, not speaking. Jobe hummed "I'll Fly Away," in time with his slow, tired steps. He took a big breath and blew it out in a white cloud lit by the lights from Lorelei's house, one shining out on the road from her front window, one in the back. He shoved his hands down in his jacket pockets and looked at me through the dimness. He tried to smile.

I had to say it. "Jobe, I figured when you went to church, you'd be sitting there by Raynell, maybe sometimes praying for me. But the snakes, Jobe?"

He sighed. "They won't hurt me unless I'm meant to be hurt. Handlers get bit all the time. Most live through it, some get sick, and some die. It's all in His hands."

I shook his arm. "You were just lucky tonight. They'll bite you. Right, Papa?"

I wanted Papa to agree, to say for sure Jobe couldn't get the snakes out again, but he didn't. "Papa?"

"Pert," he said, grief staining his voice. "At first I couldn't understand it, but somehow it makes sense to me now — as much sense as anything."

Weariness hit me. Far-off light came from our front window, but it seemed to move back into the woods instead of get closer. I put my hand on Jobe's arm and let him pull me down the road.

"I'm so tired," I whispered. I shivered in the cold air, and in my mind I saw again that old Orris snake sticking his head up over Jobe's shoulder.

"It's glory, Pert," said Jobe. "I was carried away by the glory of the moment. Didn't you feel it, too?"

"Glory? Dying of snakebite don't seem like glory to me."

Jobe put his arm around me, and we walked into our yard.

Inside, Jobe hung our jackets on pegs by the door and went into the kitchen to get us some crackers for a snack. He crossed over stripes and blocks of color. The pattern ran around the front room in a large rectangle, only a small square in the middle left bare. We had a narrow white strip right up against the walls, then wider stripes of green and diamond shapes in dusty rose, gray, smoke blue, mauve, and brick red. And in each of the four corners, one of Truly's painted scenes — a sunset over a pond, a squirrel climbing a tree, three little children playing jump rope, and an old woman sitting in a rocking chair piecing a quilt.

Jobe came back, gave me a handful of crackers, said, "Don't worry, Pert. My fate is in God's hands."

I lay down on my cot. I shut my eyes as tight as I could.

Glory may be what Jobe called it, but I knew I couldn't be satisfied to fall for anything that lasted for only a moment.

↜ Jobe ↝

Divine retribution was what I deserved for what I did to Orris and for what happened to Mama. It was what I had to live for. The Day of Judgment could fall upon my head, sudden and mighty, the sword of God. By His grace only was I spared from day to day.

Each time I raised the snakes I would have to rouse the hope and fear in me, time after time, then wait at the mercy seat of Almighty God to see if my sacrifice of faith would be accepted. If not, if my heart failed me, they would strike. They would kill me.

And if I didn't die, I'd have to keep going, keep raising the snakes, give my body as a living sacrifice all the days of my life.

I was already weary with this grace.

Empty.

How could I go on?

But how could I stop?

It was my sin. Now it was my duty to work out my salvation.

~ Pert ~

Before Papa and Jobe left for work in the morning,
Papa bent over to give me a good-bye kiss. My forehead
ached. When I remembered Jobe and the rattlesnakes,
I covered my head, then huddled down and slept until
way up in the morning. I woke at a knock on the front
door, and Lorelei's voice.

"Pert, Pert, you in there?" Lorelei knocked until I
got up and crossed the square of unpainted planks and
stripes and blocks of color and opened the door Jobe
had painted pale green.

Lorelei stepped in, her teeth chattering from the
chill winter morning, onto a bright yellow rectangle.
Papa had painted yellow fringe on each end and written
WELCOME in black letters across it. "Now ain't that
clever," she said, bending down to look closer. "Did
John think that up, or Jobe?"

"Truly did."

"I might have known." Then she turned her head sideways, put her chubby little fingers over her lips, and frowned. "What does it mean, with that 'Welcome' upside down? Makes it look like you're welcome to go out the door."

I saw the mistake, but wouldn't let on to Lorelei but what that was how Truly'd planned it.

Lorelei touched my cheek. It hurt and I brushed her hand away.

She wrinkled her nose. "Still too skinny." Lorelei sat down, adjusted her heavy self on the couch. "You need to get back to those hot school lunches and get some meat on your ribs."

I stood in front of her, getting cold.

"What about Jobe last night?" she said. "Now, wasn't that just a miracle to behold?"

I frowned.

"Have you ever seen anyone so full of faith and not a bit afraid? You could just see it — Jobe has the authority to be an evangelist."

I stepped backward away from her. "Nobody better try to make one out of him, is all I can say."

Lorelei caught her breath. "Least you could do is give him a little encouragement. Poor boy," she said, and sat up straighter. "He's doing everything he can to help you."

I picked up my quilt, wrapped it around me, and lay down, all my energy gone again.

"I saw you with that Nunn boy last night. I just think poor Truly would want you to think again about him. His past of stealing may not be in his past, you know."

I just lay there.

What did she know about what Truly would think?

Lorelei said, "This cold weather throws my hens off. And lately some have come up missing. I hope they're not going sickly. I haven't noticed them molting and moping around. Likely somebody's been swiping them's my take on it."

I wouldn't even say one word. What would Elwayne want with her old chickens?

"Your hens laying good?"

"I don't know," I said, not even opening my eyes. "You can go see for yourself."

She went through the kitchen and on out. The door slammed. I got up, crossed over to the window, and watched as she walked along the path between our houses. Round in her quilted nylon coat and wool head-scarf, she never even glanced at the hens clucking around her feet.

Lorelei disappeared into the woods, leaving nothing out there but bare trees, yellow grass, and chickens.

The house got too quiet. I crept to the other windows and peeked out.

Orris could be out there, just on the other side of these walls. From the front window I could see only a little ways down the road back toward Sardis, and from the window on my side of the room, I could see the bend in the road and, through the trees, the worn wood houses around the circle of Lexieville. Not even a car went by to disturb the peace and quiet.

Elwayne wouldn't steal Lorelei's chickens. But Orris, hiding out in the woods and hungry, he'd steal them for sure. The sureness of it grew around me, the air filled with it.

For a half hour, I watched and waited, sat covered up on my cot. I could almost hear him breathing, and when the chickens clucked and fluttered around, my heart nearly stopped in my chest. No matter how much he wanted to finish up with me, surely he wouldn't dare come here. But he might.

I checked and locked the doors again, then peeked under the kitchen sink to see if Papa's hunting knife was still there, and tried to calm down. I couldn't stay here anymore, not alone like this. I'd have to go back to school. I dug around in the cardboard box I kept under my cot until I found a shampoo sample that'd come in the mail, then I struck a match to light the kitchen stove, heated up a kettle of water, and poured it into our big dishpan. I bent forward and let my hair settle into the warm water. I scooped the water with my hand and poured it over the back of my head.

My body relaxed a little. I dribbled the pearly pink shampoo into my hand, and it smelled like strawberry ice cream. I squeezed suds through my hair, then rinsed with warm water right out of the kettle. Steam rose from the pan, around my face, into the cold room.

When my spine shivered, like someone else could be in the room, I wrapped my head in a towel and raised up. The usual salt-pork odor of the kitchen had changed to strawberries. I toweled my hair and walked around the front room, and even the old dirt smell got covered up.

In a corner pile of dirty clothes, I dug around until I found a pair of jeans and a red sweatshirt. Back in the kitchen, I gave myself a sponge bath, then washed my clothes in the shampoo water and hung them to dry on chairs pulled up close to the open oven. Dressed in one of Lorelei's old flannel gowns, I put on my jacket, propped myself up on the couch by the front door, and tried to read my overdue library book. In it this man looked out a castle window and saw a woman's pale, ghostly face. He was sick with love for her, but she was dead.

Elwayne came over to check on me after school. He reminded me that I hadn't taken a ride yet in the car his dad had helped him buy. He told me all about it while he made a peanut butter sandwich and I combed my hair in front of the oven. When it'd almost dried, he reached over and lifted a strand to his nose. "Strawberries," he said, and grinned like he smelled real summer berries.

"I wish it was summer," I said.

He nodded. "I'll pick you some strawberries when summer comes."

I wanted summer and strawberries and Elwayne again, but first I had to get through the winter with Truly gone and Orris out there somewhere. As soon as Papa and Jobe got there, I told Elwayne he could go on home. I asked him for a ride to school the next day, and he grinned.

Papa and Jobe had brought us a brick of chili and some rat cheese for supper. When Jobe heard my news about going back to school, he rubbed his hands together and started cooking. I could tell he thought the snakes had done the trick, and I wished I'd had the courage to stay home a few more days. But I didn't.

"You need a good hot supper before you go back tomorrow," Papa said, and stirred in a spoonful of pinto beans from the pot he'd cooked yesterday for Sunday dinner. The chili's spice filled the kitchen.

Before I went to bed, I rearranged my half-dried clothes, and Jobe gave me a hug and said, "You're sure looking pretty to go back to school."

I went to check the mirror beside the back door to see if what he said was true, but what with the room being so dim and the old spots on the mirror, I couldn't tell. Maybe I'd look again in the morning.

I didn't know what I looked like anymore.

➣ Pert ➣

Jobe's cot springs creaked and his feet hit the floor. "Better get on up, Pert. Elwayne'll be here in half a hour." Then he headed for the kitchen, where Papa was cooking something.

With a sour sleep taste in my mouth, I ran my fingers through my fine-scented hair and snagged them on tangles, reached for my comb on the windowsill, then sat up and started in. It might take the whole half-hour just to get the tangles out. The chill air in the house seeped into the stretched elastic at the wrists of my flannel gown, and gave me goose bumps.

Papa came through the kitchen door and grinned at me. "I fixed you some grits and honey," he said, "and your clothes are all dry. You can go stand in front of the stove to get dressed where you'll be warm."

I threw back my covers and hurried toward the warmth of the kitchen, stopping only to hug Papa there in the doorway. The top of my head came up to his chin. He bent his head over mine and smoothed my hair.

He breathed in and said, "That's a pretty smell."

When we looked at each other, I thought he saw I was a little nervous about school, and he looked down at me like he'd never seen anything so perfect.

"Thanks, Papa." I went in to dress in my warm stiff jeans and strawberry-smelling sweatshirt. He went outside to try to get the pickup started and warmed up.

Jobe, at the kitchen table, held a cup of coffee between his rough-skinned hands. My coffee and grits sat across from him. "I'm glad you're going back to school today," he said.

"Well, it's better than being here all alone," I said through my first warm, lumpy bite of grits. "Who knows where Orris is."

Jobe frowned a little, stood up, took his coffee, and went to the back window. He pushed aside the curtain I'd made a few years ago from a square of material strung along a piece of twine nailed to each side of the window. Jobe went real still and tense, craned his neck, and stared out into the gray-lit woods. My heart thumped.

I dropped my spoon into the grits bowl. "What's out there, Jobe?"

"Nothing, Pert. Probably just a deer. Too misty to tell."

He turned back to the stove and made like to stir up the grits in the pan. Any day now Orris could show up again, just like that.

Elwayne pulled up outside, his muffler sounding like sobs, and prickles stung the back of my eyes. I didn't want to, but I had to get ready to face Elwayne and school. I said to Jobe, "What Truly used to say about you and Papa was right. You're good."

Jobe's face crumpled, and he ran a hand across his forehead. "I beat Orris up pretty bad."

"I'm glad," I whispered. "I hope he's hurting."

I turned and went through the front room, stepped outside across the yellow-painted welcome mat, and rode off in Elwayne's old green car.

For a while there I had a little trouble with my breath. I held it, eased it out, in and out, as we drove past Lorelei's, the mission, the flakeboard dump, then on up the road past where Orris caught me coming home from school.

Elwayne looked sideways at me. "You all right, Pert?"

"Sure," I said, surprised at how normal I sounded. "A little nervous, is all."

At school, a double line of long yellow buses filled the circle drive in front with the stink of exhaust fumes and noise: the squawk of worn brakes, shouts, and laughter from the kids who poured from the bus doors. Even from the parking lot at the side, it overpowered me.

I almost got back in Elwayne's car, but Elwayne had ahold of my arm and guided me up the sidewalk to the side door. When he opened it, warm air and the smell of the hallway blew out, and on top of it all came the biscuits-and-eggs fragrance of the breakfast all us from Lexieville, who couldn't afford it, got for free.

Even though I'd already had breakfast, I managed to eat two biscuits, an egg, and a sausage patty. I hadn't realized I was so hungry.

Elwayne walked me to the office, said, "See you in the funny papers," and went on down the hall like he owned the place. He turned the corner and left me there. He peeked back around the corner and made a funny face at me, waved his hand like *Get on in there*. So I got up the courage and went in. I nearly ran into Mr. Banes just outside his office.

"Pert," he said, sounding like he was my best friend. "I'm glad to see you're back."

I said, "I just need a pass to get in class."

Mr. Banes scribbled on a pink slip of paper. He smiled when he handed it to me, like this would make all my dreams come true. "Why don't you sign up on the counselor's schedule before you go?" he said. "You might want someone to talk to."

"No, thanks," I said. "I already got a social worker. Mrs. Turnbull."

He nodded. "You've got a friend in her," he said, and let me go on to class.

I thought I might not make it through the morning, but I did, even through second-period home ec when Brittany Lee gave her term-project presentation, "Decorative Stitchery for the Holiday Home."

I was glad when lunch came and Elwayne, Raynell, and I sat down together at a table off in the corner. Brittany Lee, in the middle of the middle table, handed out big green jingle bells on red cords — necklaces to be worn by all her friends during the month of December. For a second, I imagined I sat across from her, and that she put one right in my hand.

We finished lunch, and Elwayne, Raynell, and I had to walk by her table to take our trays back. No one even glanced up. It was like they couldn't be bothered to even notice us, much less gossip about us anymore. I guess what Orris'd done outdid anything Brittany Lee could imagine about Lexies. I'd finally become invisible.

Before I hardly knew it, the day'd passed and I stood at my locker, Elwayne coming down the hall toward me. Brittany Lee walked a ways in front of him. I didn't expect her to see me, so I watched her. But she cut her eyes over toward me, and wrinkled up her nose a little.

She went a couple more steps past me, but then turned, and her eyes had this look, a look I never ever wanted to see there: pity. "Pert," she said, like she just had to tell me something, like she cared. But she stopped when she saw Elwayne and went on to the door.

Elwayne and I glanced at each other. He said, "What's with her?"

"I don't know." I leaned my forehead against his chest. The picture of her face stayed in my head. She'd never have been my friend, but now we couldn't even be enemies anymore, either. Worse than being nothing, worse than being invisible, was that Brittany Lee Hathaway now felt sorry for me. I just wanted to sink down on this green-and-white-swirled linoleum and sleep.

Elwayne and I went out and got in his car.

"You okay?" Elwayne said.

"Maybe I went back to school too soon," I whispered. "I'm so tired." I rested my head on the back of the seat. My stomach rolled.

The car shook and bumped back through Lexieville

to my house, where I leaned over and made myself give Elwayne a kiss on the cheek.

As if he could tell I'd had to force it, he looked down at his hands on the wheel and said, "You going tomorrow?"

"I'll try. If I can get some rest tonight," I said. I checked to see if anyone was around before I opened the door and got out, then hurried on inside back across the upside-down welcome mat, locked the door behind me, fell on my cot, and slept, still in my coat.

I could tell before I opened my eyes it was evening. Muffled voices, Papa's and Jobe's, came from beyond the kitchen door, along with the dull clatter of dishes and forks. A steady rain tapped the tin roof. I opened my eyes a little, and before I could think, I glanced over to see if Truly was napping, too. The gray day deepened to near dark. I just wanted to sleep, never think about anything again. I lay there and listened to the rain come down. There ought to be some dreary background music: "Rainy Night in Georgia," but I figured a rainy night in Arkansas'd even beat one in Georgia for sadness.

Papa went out the back door, and Jobe came in the front room.

"Pert," Jobe whispered from the doorway. "You awake?"

"Yeah," I said, and went to sit up. I scooted back, slow, slow, and leaned up against the wall. My head still ached. The newspapers, soggy from damp, didn't even crackle.

Jobe came over and sat at the foot of my cot. "I need to talk to you, Pert. I got some things on my mind."

"What about?" I could just make out Jobe's face in the dimness of the room.

"Some things I hate to bring up to you." His soft voice shook. "But I can't stand it anymore."

"Jobe, you and me can talk about anything."

His shadowy face looked pulled over his bones. Love for him rushed in my chest, so I leaned forward and touched his face, said, "Go on, tell me."

He grabbed my hand between both of his and held tight. "Pert, I'm no better than he was. What he did to you — I've done lots worse to him." His voice caught on a sob and he stopped.

My scalp tingled.

He struggled to start again. "I beat him up bad. Real bad." The windblown rain scattered across our roof. "Pert, I killed him."

My heart pumped hard. Neither of us moved for a moment. I rejoiced. I was free of Orris.

Jobe leaned into me. Rain pounded the roof and

poured down the windowpanes. I held him, and his tears soaked through my sweatshirt, warm and wet against my skin.

The whole world dimmed down like the rainy night around me, and I saw that big snake wrap around Jobe's neck, flick his tongue to taste the air, then turn and pierce me with his icy eyes. My rejoicing was over. I saw it all now. The price for my freedom was Jobe. Orris had him now.

My throat stung, my lungs burned, but I couldn't cry.

I rocked Jobe back and forth, said, "It was self-defense. The sheriff, Mrs. Turnbull, everybody'll be able to see that. They won't put you in jail."

He pulled away from me. "Jail?" he said, like it'd never occurred to him, like it meant nothing. "It's a *sin,* Pert, a mortal sin."

Jobe paused, cleared his throat, and spoke, his voice hoarse. "You got to listen and try to understand. There's only one way out."

Sick with it, I whispered, "The snakes?"

"I'm called — now just listen a minute," he said as if I'd tried to interrupt. "I don't know if I would have been if it weren't for what happened with Orris. But now I know my only redemption is to give myself to it and let Cusper teach me how to preach."

"Jobe, jail'd be better, safer than those snakes."

"You want me to go to jail?"

"No, course I don't."

That rain had poured a lake between us.

I crossed my arms. "I didn't sin. Orris was the devil himself."

Jobe stood up. His voice was old and tired. "Well, I sinned."

"Jobe, maybe it's not a sin to kill the devil."

Jobe went over to his cot and lay down. "Orris was just a man, Pert. Like any other. It's hard enough just to be decent. Not good, even."

He sighed, and in a whisper probably meant for himself alone, he said, "I wanted to be good."

I sank into my cot. All the air in our front room pressed down on me. Lord, was it raining all over the world?

Jobe would never forget Cusper and the snakes, not if he carried the cross of Orris's death. I hoped Orris was dead for my own sake, but something in me resisted, and I prayed he was alive for Jobe's sake. Inside my head I called to Jobe, like he walked far away down the road. I wanted to get up and go over to him in the night, say, "Are you awake, Jobe? Are you there?" I wanted to hold on to him, put my thoughts in his head and drown out Cusper's. My thoughts moved and shifted, tried to find their way to him, but his sorrow and guilt rose up like a wall between us. I wanted to say, Maybe you didn't kill him, maybe he's alive. Hope and fear raced into me and something deep whispered back, "Maybe Orris *is* alive."

The December night settled around us, quiet and cold. Papa's, Jobe's, and my breath never even began to warm it.

⇒ Pert ⇐

I had to save Jobe. I had to go into Vernal and face Mrs. Turnbull and tell her I wasn't going to Little Rock anymore. At the start of winter break I brought out my old paint clothes, shook them, and dressed from head to toe in white. Just like old times, Papa, Jobe, and I climbed into the truck cab and drove off — except now, Truly wasn't there to wave us away.

I got a catch in my breath.

"You cold, Pert?" Jobe asked.

"Naw," I said, and slid down in the seat and pretended to nap until we drove in at the welfare office.

When I went into Mrs. Turnbull's office, she waved me to a chair. She sat down and picked up her pen. "How are you, Pert?" she said, her voice kind, her eyes searching out mine.

I gazed down into my lap, where I held my hands clasped tight between my knees. "Fine." She wouldn't believe me until I met her eyes. I glanced up. This light brought out lines around her eyes I hadn't noticed before.

"I hear Jobe and Raynell plan to get married." Mrs. Turnbull smiled.

"I guess." I released my hands and rubbed the palms across my knees.

"Your father tells me Raynell comes in and helps around the house." She paused like I might argue.

"She's helping out some."

Mrs. Turnbull leaned back a little in her chair. "I'm glad your father and Jobe will have someone to help them out when you go off to school."

"Mrs. Turnbull, I have something to tell you."

"What is it, Pert?"

"I decided I'm not going to Little Rock, not this summer, anyway."

Mrs. Turnbull raised her eyebrows. "Not going?"

"I can't leave Papa and Jobe." My pulse beat too loud in my ears. I got almost dizzy with what I'd done.

She frowned. Then her face smoothed out, and it crossed my mind that she'd try to talk me out of it. That made me feel even worse. I couldn't leave them. Not even if what I suspected deep inside was true and

151

Orris was alive. Not even if someday I'd have to come face to face with him again.

Mrs. Turnbull put her hands flat on her desk, stood up, and leaned toward me. She opened her mouth, shut it again. She came around to sit beside me and rested her hand on my shoulder. "You are enrolled in the class that begins June fifteenth."

Her face, tight and pale, gave me an ache in the middle of my chest. I said, "Maybe next year, after I know they will do okay without me."

Mrs. Turnbull almost whispered, "Someone else who graduates next year may qualify ahead of you. Don't miss your opportunity, Pert."

"But Jobe?" I said, imagining those rattlesnakes in his hands.

Mrs. Turnbull snapped, "Jobe's soon to be married."

"Papa . . ."

Mrs. Turnbull, less sharp now, got quieter and firmer. "Your papa wouldn't want you to miss out on this, Pert. You know that."

"But he's so sad. Truly . . ." Her name took all my words away.

Mrs. Turnbull said, "Oh, Pert, neither one of them would expect you to change your plans. If you could ask your mother she would tell you so."

The ache spread into my stomach.

Mrs. Turnbull went to her desk. She steepled her hands and pointed her two fingers at me. "Don't decide right now. Your deposit is already paid, your place is reserved, so take your time and think."

I tried to make my face hard as stone, but inside, part of me leaned toward her.

"You'd better go on to work now." Mrs. Turnbull opened a folder and made notes. She didn't look up, no smile, no good-bye. But she didn't sound mad, just real, real serious.

When I left, I walked by Katie. She glanced up but kept on typing. I got my painter's cap off the coat rack, went out, and headed down the sidewalk toward the health department building.

I tried not to, but I couldn't help it. I imagined the sidewalks in Little Rock full of men and women in suits and shiny shoes who rushed through the revolving doors of tall mirrored buildings and into shops full of summer clothes. And there I would be, walking along with five or six other new graduates, our hair shiny blond and black and red, all fixed up. College boys working at their part-time delivery jobs would stop and watch us go by on our way to McDonald's for lunch. They would wonder how they might manage to make our acquaintance. Then, blotting out Little Rock, the image of Lexieville rose up, Elwayne, Papa, Jobe, and Raynell all sitting around the kitchen table. Jobe, somehow safe and sound, was no longer bound by those snakes, and I was putting a pan of cornbread down in front of them. How he escaped, my imagination didn't show me, but I knew I'd had a hand in it.

When I got to the Spring County Health Department and opened the door, the smell of medicine mixed with new paint jarred me. Near the back of the building a tall wooden ladder was spread open across the hallway, and Papa hung on up there, his paint roller full of ceiling white. Below him, Jobe bent over a new five-gallon plastic bucket, popped off its lid, and dipped into it with an extra-long stirring stick. Tenderness and sorrow filled me.

They had drop cloths on the floor and a couple of other ladders set up at the end of the hall. I climbed toward the ceiling on one of them, and Jobe handed me up a paint pan and roller. He didn't even look at me. Tiny cracks ran across the ceiling like a crazy road map or a million snakes scratched into the old paint. I dipped the roller into the tray and watched the pale yellow plush soak up the white paint and shine with it. I raised the roller toward the ceiling, and paint spattered like rain on the canvas below.

I had to find a way to save Jobe.

I covered my patch of ceiling with a thick cloud of

new paint, imagined an airplane trying to find its way through the clouds to the earth below. I rolled out a thick white rain to cover the world, hid all the pain under one layer, then another and another. Hid all the pain and painted away the snakes.

That evening on my cot, covered with the quilt, I watched the sky darken and worked on my courage until Jobe came back from Raynell's. A cabinet door tapped in the kitchen, and I peeked in to make sure it was him before I slid around the threshold. He jumped.

"Jobe," I whispered, "Papa told me you'd be raising up the rattlers this Sunday." I touched his arm, and he pulled it away. That hurt, but not enough to stop the certainty growing in me. "You wouldn't have to if Orris was alive."

He looked down at the table. "Pert, I know what happened out there."

"But you don't know what happened after you left."

"He wasn't moving, and I buried him in the leaves."

"Jobe, Truly always tried to tell me Orris didn't really mean no harm. I didn't believe her, but she believed everything she said, didn't she?"

"I guess so."

"Remember how she told us the dumplings were for Orris? She'd believed that. Why would she say that unless she really believed it, unless she thought he was alive?"

"She was confused in her head, Mrs. Turnbull said."

"Maybe so, but maybe not. What if she wasn't as bad off as everybody thought? What if she'd seen him alive?"

He shook his head.

My heart beat faster. "How can you be sure?"

His voice gruff and his chin set, Jobe said, "I know the truth, Pert."

"Then you show me where he is. I need to know it, too," I said, and I was there again, dried leaves rattling in the breeze. The taste of blood and dirt. Orris.

Jobe studied the palms of his hands, then jumped up, grabbed the flashlight, and he was out the door. I had to nearly run to keep up with him as he hurried down the road in the dusky light.

We found the place where Orris'd chased me, the broken branch I'd tried to grab. We turned into the forest, stepped through underbrush haunted now by Orris. I took Jobe's hand, and he led me past where I'd nearly seen my death. Something in the air rose around me and sent a tremor all through me. Jobe held my hand tighter, pulled me closer to him. Through the shadowy trees ahead, the end of the sunset slipped away behind us and night started.

"There," Jobe said, and stopped.

We stood above a low spot at the base of an oak

whose roots ran like branches along the ground. Jobe pointed at a mound of leaves held down by a fallen limb.

"Okay." I couldn't move.

"It's getting dark." Jobe opened his hand, but I held tight. He shook me loose, stepped down, and bent over the leaves. He tossed the limb off and reached into the leaves.

"Jobe!"

He jumped back. "What?"

I bent double. My chest hurt me.

Jobe touched my shoulder. "Pert," he said, his voice thick like he could cry. "Are you all right?"

Behind him, a light flashed. A pinpoint, like a cigarette lighter, and an orangey highlighted face. Orange skin, black sunken shadow sockets.

Orris's face. Orris, dead or alive, I couldn't tell. Just a flash, there and gone. I dug my nails into Jobe's shoulders. I wanted to scream, but I had no voice, only panting and a whisper.

"Jobe, someone's watching," I hissed.

Jobe peered into the woods, ready to fight. "Where?" he whispered.

I pointed to where an orange glow wavered behind the new leaves and pine boughs, to where an oval moon rose in the blue-black sky.

"The moon," I said. Only the rising moon.

"The battery's getting low. We'd better hurry." Jobe bent over the leaves again.

"Not your hands, Jobe. Use a stick or something. Don't touch him with your hands."

Jobe broke a forked branch off the fallen limb and poked into the leaves, stirred them, raked and scattered them. Nothing but leaves.

"Maybe animals got him," I said. Now I wanted him to be there. If not, he was probably watching us right that minute.

"No bones, nor nothing. This must not be the place."

"Jobe, maybe you didn't kill him."

"I *did* kill him." He threw down the stick and grabbed my arm. He pulled me backward into a little more light.

Fear crept up out of those leaves, along my arms, to the back of my neck. Jobe shone his flashlight all around and searched the trees, his breath coming faster. His body, tense and electric now, leaped away, pulled me with it, and we ran like something horrible was after us. We zigzagged through the trees while it came straight and clawed at the hem of my shirt.

We broke through to the road, pounded through the ruts past the dump, past the empty church, past

Lorelei's. Away down the road, car lights came toward us. We ran for home.

We huddled at the kitchen table till we calmed down so as not to wake Papa, then went in to try to sleep.

After that, Jobe wouldn't talk about Orris at all. He grew quieter, spent more time with Cusper and Pansy at the church, spent less time at home or with Raynell. What I'd done was make things worse for Jobe. And all but convince myself Orris still lived on the same earth as me. Jobe would keep on with the snakes till they killed him. Papa wouldn't do anything, and Raynell couldn't. I was the only one.

⇒ Jobe ⇐

I prayed nearly all night every night trying not to give false hope any chance in my heart. But I couldn't help it. I wanted him alive. I wanted Orris back. When I finally fell to sleep and dreaming, there was Raynell, taking the snakes from my hands and raising them up in a sunlit forest. As she touched them, they turned into white birds with blue wings and flew away. She gathered me up in her arms, kissed my hair.

I remembered that kiss when I walked into the house after work today, and there she came from the kitchen to meet me with my mama's wooden spoon in her hand. She'd spread up the beds with their quilts and draped one over the couch, even stashed the dirty clothes some-where besides our usual corner.

Papa, right behind me, said, "Evening, Raynell," just

like he'd been coming in the door and seeing her for years.

"Evening, Mr. Lexie," she said. "I thought you all might like some stew I fixed last night. I've brought you the extry so it wouldn't go to waste."

Papa sniffed and grinned. "Smells good, don't you say so, Jobe?"

I took off my hat and walked over to give her a hello kiss. Her eyes looked worried, and I whispered, "Thank you."

She relaxed then, almost like she'd been afraid she'd done something wrong. Right then, all I wanted was Orris alive. I wanted a normal life — with Raynell and suppers and kids.

We went into the kitchen and sat down at the table.

Papa said, "Well now, Raynell, this is mighty good of ye."

Raynell blushed.

The back door opened and Pert came in, looked around like she didn't recognize the place, and frowned at Raynell. "What's going on?"

Papa pushed her a chair out with his foot. "Dinner's ready," he said. "Have yourself a seat."

Pert thumped down in the chair and clamped her jaw shut. Raynell set a bowl in front of her. And she ate, all quiet and still. I forced myself to chew and swallow. If Orris was alive, nothing would be normal; he'd just try to hurt Pert again. While Papa and Raynell talked about painting and school, I thought about poison and prayed.

⇐ Pert ⇐

Saturday night, wide awake on my cot, I waited. After Papa and Jobe went to bed, after their breathing'd been slow and even for a long time, I got up. I didn't get my jacket, just grabbed my quilt and crept, trembling, into the kitchen in the dark, and I took Papa's hunting knife from under the sink, just in case. I knew what I had to do: set those snakes free, so Jobe'd be free. I had to go even if Orris could be out there somewhere. I tiptoed to the back door, my heart so loud I felt sure they'd hear it and wake up. I almost hoped they would.

Just outside the back door, I paused for a minute to see if I'd roused anyone. I listened toward the woods, then when all was quiet, I covered my head with my quilt and went on out to the road.

At the back door of the mission, nothing seemed real, not the moonlight's blue glow off the white church, not my pale blue-nailed fingers. The doorknob burned cold as it turned in my palm. A crack of darkness opened in the wall. The door swung open, all silence on top of silence, and I stepped into the blackness.

A faint shift of rattle. The snakes knew I was there. I bumped a chair. My knees buckled, and I sat, the chair's metal cool on my legs. My eyes adjusted, and a heater glowed red near the crates, keeping the snakes' blood moving, even in the winter cold.

I stood. The quilt dropped off my shoulders, plunked against the metal seat, then slithered to the floor. I crept toward the crate I'd seen Cusper put the two smaller snakes in. I tried to raise the crate off the floor without disturbing the snakes, but halfway up it bumped the other and their rattles howled. I dropped the crate. From both crates came hisses and thumps.

After a while, the crates got quiet again and my blood slowed down.

I eased the crate up by its handle again, slowly, slowly. It didn't bump the other one this time, but floated up under my hand. I tiptoed to the door and walked out a ways into the moonlit woods and set it down under a pine tree.

I went back for the larger crate and floated it out

the door and off in the opposite direction. I leaned over to set it down on the ground, but the weight inside shifted, the crate tipped forward, and the rattles clattered against the sides. I dropped the crate and ran.

Inside the church, I huddled under my quilt as near the heater as I could get without catching myself afire. A cold reptile smell hovered in the room.

While the snakes' blood congealed in the chill night air, I waited and warmed and nodded. Almost asleep, I roused myself and hurried outside. The smaller crate glowed in the moonlight. I eased it over on its side. The hinge latch had no padlock, so I slipped Papa's knife out of its leather case and, with the pointed silver blade, flipped the latch. The lid clattered open and straw and snakes spilled out. I held my knife ready. The two snakes crawled away, one twisting and hiding along a tree root, the other shushing through the pine needles to disappear into shadow.

I latched the crate and carried it back inside to its place beside the heater, then looked out toward the spot where I had dropped the other crate. Darkness. That crate had disappeared into the moon shadow of a black tree trunk. Even so, I could almost see those Orris eyes. They watched me through a slit in the wood. The moon, on its way down, would soon leave nothing but black night, when even the trees disappeared.

I clutched the knife. I wanted it done. I hurried over. In the dark, my foot crashed against something. The crate. I stumbled. The lid slapped open. I fell just as the snake hit the ground, rattles loud in the cold night. My hand landed on its belly, and the snake slid under my palm. Its slow rattle told me which end to fear, and before it could raise its head to follow my warmth, I struck out with the knife in my other hand. My blade glanced off its hide. I stabbed again and again. The blade wouldn't slice through its tough skin. Its tail wrapped around my left arm. I screamed and stabbed at its head, and the blade slid into flesh. Its body relaxed and fell to the ground. The rattles clicked together, then were silent.

The moon'd gone now. I panted and gasped, lay there, and let the night own us for a while. When the cold changed, and the dawn breeze brushed the tops of the trees, I carried the crate back inside. I held my hands to the warmth of the heater for a minute, then picked up my quilt and started toward the road. Gray light showed in the east.

Over by the bush the snake lay dead, that knife sunk to its handle inside its open mouth. Joy washed over me. I'd done it. I bent and pulled the knife out and took the rattle in my hand. Its hard jointed segments made their dry clacks. I dropped it in the dust and put the knife away, wiped my hands on my jeans.

Then I pulled the quilt down past my forehead and went on down the rutty road home.

That morning, I wanted to see the expression on everybody's faces once they saw the snakes had up and disappeared. So I snuck in to services after they'd got started and watched from the vestibule. I hid over to the side of the entrance during the last trailing notes of a hymn. Then came Cusper's preaching voice.

"It takes FAITH, brethren," he shouted. Then a little quieter: "Faith, as a mustard seed." Whispering now, he said, "Faith, as of a little child. Show us your faith, young Brother Jobe."

"Amen, amen," the people said, and I peeked at Jobe going up there, his Bible hugged close. My whole chest filled with love for him.

Jobe's voice, nearly too quiet, coming like it did after Cusper's loudness, sounded hoarse. Jobe said, "I've been asked to say a few words before we bring out the evidence of our faith." He laid his Bible down and shuffled around a bit. Finally, he dropped his hand down onto the pulpit. The thump roused him a bit. "Like as of a child . . ." He seemed to be thinking it over. "Faith like that can serve to move mountains or" — he paused — "or shut the mouths of deadly vipers." Jobe looked over at the crates and everybody looked over there, too. They listened, but, of course, there wasn't even a rustle.

Jobe cleared his throat. "Verily, I say that what Cusper's scripture meant was that we like to have to be pure in heart, and if not that, at least holding a heart of trust, the way a child does looking up at grownups around her." Jobe's gaze traveled over the congregation, and for a second I thought he'd spotted me. I ducked back.

"And woe be to anybody messing with that trust!" He stopped and sniffed. Sounded like he might be about to cry. "We each one of us needs to go back deep inside to find that faith we were born with."

I was watching again as he balled up his fist and brought it down on the pulpit, but it made almost no sound. "I don't know about you, but I vow to find the courage now and, Lord willing, ever' day to come."

"Praise Jesus," the people said, as Jobe turned and approached the crates. Cusper hopped up and went to assist. Pansy crashed down on the piano keys, and the people sang out, stood, and clapped. Jobe and Cusper knelt down by the crates. Jobe put his hands on Cusper's shoulders. Cusper covered Jobe's head with his hands. Then they bowed their heads and Cusper prayed.

"Lord!" His voice rang off the rafters. "Lord, we beseech Thee. Lord, let Your power and Jobe's faith and the faith of each one here bind these beasts of hell. Shut the vipers' mouths! Save Your servant Jobe! Even today, Lord. We beg and beseech. Show us the way, O Lord, amen."

"Yes, Lord," Lorelei said. Others whispered, "Sweet Jesus, Lord, show us the way."

Pansy's music lifted and rang through the room. A few danced in the aisles, clapped their hands, tapped their shoes on the board floor. Echoes and heat bounced around the room.

Cusper and Jobe laid their hands on the crates. Their lips moving in prayer, they bent together to raise the lids. We all held our breath as they peeked inside, then gaped at each other.

"They're gone," Jobe said.

Cusper whirled around to face the people. "What does this mean?"

Lorelei waved her hands above her head. "A miracle."

Cusper said, "Delivered by the angel of the Lord! This trial is over, Brother Jobe. So be it."

Jobe's eyes went big and deep and dark, and he looked up and straight at me. Jobe said, "What now?"

"Now?" Cusper's face changed, as if something bad was dawning on him right then. His shoulders sagged, then Cusper pulled himself together and stood up straight.

"As soldiers of the faith, Brother Jobe and I have girded ourselves in preparation for this time. One trial may be past, but another looms ahead."

What was he talking about?

Jobe rubbed his lips with his fingers.

Cusper sighed. "The ultimate test of faith, my brothers and sisters, is upon us. Whether this be the work of Jehovah or Satan, this evening's service will show. When we all gather together again tonight, young Jobe and I will drink from the cup of death and be unharmed. Tonight, my friends, we'll be able to drink the deadliest poison and yet live. Until then, Jobe and I will remain here in prayer and supplication."

≈ Pert ≈

I ran out of the church and all the way home. On my cot, I shivered under the quilt, weeping and wailing for what I'd gone and done now. I saw Truly again, pale and dying in the grass; Jobe in a cold sweat banging his head against the outhouse wall and retching.

The only thing could save him now was Orris alive.

I searched the patchwork-painted floorboards. Where Papa had painted light colors, I could see no snakes, but in the corners, under the beds, and on the painted patches, I couldn't be sure. I heard their little sounds — clicks, rattles, low hisses. I strained my eyes to see, and in the deepest, darkest patches, I thought I saw a reflection of light, the glint of an eye.

I threw the quilt off and lay straight and stiff, listening. Only the sigh of wind in the treetops and the low rumble of thunder up from the west as a storm blew in. Where was Papa? He should have been back by now. The window rattled. Only the wind. I was almost sure. I rolled off my cot onto the snaky floor, my eyes watching the window. It clattered. A flash of lightning showed me nothing, nothing there. The first rain spats hit the house, and in the next flash, spots and streaks blurred the glass. Guided by the lightning, I crawled into the kitchen and opened the cabinet under the sink. I moved my hand across the mice-littered newspapers and found the leather case with Papa's knife in it.

Back in the front room, I knelt by my cot and waited. The storm crashed over my head, shook all the windows, and banged on the door.

Orris could be out there, still alive — my fear and my hope.

I watched and waited until the rain stopped, and still Papa hadn't come home. He must have stayed on with Jobe and Cusper, but I knew he wouldn't be trying to talk sense into them. Papa wasn't going to save Jobe.

A little sunlight cut a tiny hole in the clouds and sent a weak beam onto the floor. By that light I could see there were no snakes in this room. I grabbed hold of the idea that maybe one bit of luck, like that little beam of sun, could make all the difference. It might even mean that somehow I could get enough courage to do the only thing that would save Jobe, to go out there looking for Orris.

I got my jacket, put the knife in my pocket, and went out. As I turned to pull the back door shut, the cool room seemed to hold a whisper. I rested my hand on the unpainted door and leaned in to try to catch the words, but a breeze fluttered the trees behind me and covered any other sound. I closed the door and turned toward the woods.

The path took me past the big rock in the clearing, mossy and rusty with lichen but solid. Like a warning. Ahead, the trees thickened. Halfway between rock and trees I stopped, afraid to go past my last boundary to enter that place where no path guided me.

Truly and Papa used to say, "Don't go yonder of the big rock," so of course I had gone a few times, but not without an acorn of fear. When we were kids and Jobe and I'd dared venture a few steps beyond, we'd race back, panting and puffing, and hold tight to that rock. A couple times one summer, though, we'd gone with Orris out to check up on some traps he'd set in the woods, and he showed us places he used to hide from his daddy when he was a little boy. Now I had to try to find them again, find Orris. Alone.

Under thick, dripping branches, the air clung dank and clammy to my skin. A patch of weak sunshine glowed up ahead, and I scurried there. For a moment I stood in its beams, caught in a cage made of forest.

Then I made my way by the smell of damp and decay, by feel and memory, by certain knowledge. If Orris was out there, I would find him.

Wandering hour after hour under the clearing sky, I found his old hiding places, one by one. I stepped slow and quiet, made the suck of mud only a whisper when it tried to pull my feet down into the earth. As sunset came and dusk gathered, I knew I was closing in on him; I could almost smell him.

A sharp, quick sound to my left. Another and another — sneezes. And a light, a chink of yellow just ahead. Everything we'd all ever said or done thundered down to a point just above my head, then burst like a light behind my eyes.

I eased the knife from its case in my pocket and checked the blade. A tremor began in my stomach, and I crept forward. He coughed. Still I couldn't see him.

Just ahead, several saplings and small-boled trees seemed to grow sideways, with sticks woven straight up and down, leaving only a few gaps in between — a fence, made so it looked almost like the forest. A shadow moved in the gaps. I knelt and placed my eye against the split of light. The fence enclosed only a space of ten feet or so, a den made of flakeboard, already melting away after the rain, and woven branches covered with dead leaves and vines. A lantern, turned low, gave off a dull glow, and I spotted him. My mouth opened, but I managed not to gasp. His hair hung long and matted, and the sweaty paint clothes he still wore were streaked with filth and old blood. Orris coughed and coughed, nearly strangled in a coughing fit, hawked, spit, coughed again. He got to his knees, then pushed himself off the ground with his hands. Nearby four chickens with ragged, molty feathers pecked in the dirt. A hammer beat in my head and in my chest, and my knees lost all strength to spring. I couldn't even duck and hide; I froze.

The Orris I'd known all my life, bad as he'd been, wasn't nothing compared to this, this nightmare Orris. Maybe a dead man come back to life, maybe a monster ghost, he had built his shell here in the wet, dark woods. Orris, a creature. No longer a man.

Dizzy, I put my hands against the fence to keep my balance. The chickens scattered away from me, clucked across the dirt.

"Somebody there?" Orris wheezed.

Panic hit, and I turned to run. But a gate opened in the fence, and Orris peered out.

I leaped away, but he got me, clawed at my wrist, and grabbed me. I screamed, twisted away, and pointed the knife at him. He lost his hold on me, staggered, and fell backward through the gate.

He whimpered and curled himself away from me, his backside skinny as a little kid's. He moaned and wheezed. My arm shook, tried to rattle loose on me.

A breeze fluttered the leaves of his den, and the lantern wick nearly guttered out. Orris stirred, coughed deep, then rolled on his back, his breath ragged. The lantern light wavered again, then grew stronger and brighter. His eyes opened wide.

"Truly?" His lips barely moved. He reached toward me. "Truly, Truly, Truly," he moaned over and over.

Like a child, he lay before me, taking me for my own mother, dead and gone. I reeled from it.

"Sister," he said as his hand, weak and limp, lowered to the ground. His filthy hand. I hated that hand.

I stepped inside the fence. "She's dead," I said. "Your sister's dead."

His lips quivered. "Naw," he whispered. He fell into a coughing fit.

"What you did to me killed her," I said, and raised the knife ready to strike.

But my other hand, as if it were Truly's, lowered

176

and touched Orris's forehead. Hot, dry as dust, dry with fever.

He stopped coughing. Just his wheezy breath growing weaker.

"Pert," he said, knowing me now. His gaze rose to the knife, then came back to my face. Orris's hand lay near my foot, palm up, unresisting. He closed his eyes. Waited for my knife.

I took my hand from his forehead and backed away.

I ran through the forest, only the last faint glow of sunset to guide me. Raindrops dripped from the branches as I passed. My feet, loose-jointed, splashed mud, snapped sticks, scared away snakes.

In a tiny clearing, a breeze rippled across the water in the bowl of a stump. I paused to replace the knife in the leather case in my pocket. The wind, rising, blew pale clouds across the curved-blade moon.

I had to hurry. Evening services had already started. As I got closer to Lexieville, the sound of Pansy's piano and the congregation singing and clapping guided me to the church.

In the parking lot I cut between Cusper's pickup and a beat-up old Chevy. As I opened the door to the church and stepped inside, Cusper said, "It takes faith as of a mustard seed, but not that only. If you want to move mountains, it takes bowing to the Lord's will even if He chooses to slay you, even if He says, 'Tonight your soul shall be required of thee.'"

Cusper held a jar of cloudy liquid aloft. Beside him at the table stood Jobe.

Cusper bowed his head. "Jobe," he whispered.

Jobe, his voice too high-pitched, said, "If the faithful drink any hurtful thing, it shall not harm nor kill them." He looked down and from between the two open snake crates on the table he raised another jar.

My heart beat hard, one deep pain. I ran down the aisle, calling Jobe's name. I grabbed hold of his wrist, and poison splashed onto our hands, stinging them.

I didn't let go. "No, Jobe."

Then, loud enough for him to hear over Cusper and the crowd, but quiet enough to keep his secret, I said, "Orris is alive."

He jerked back, and hope stirred in his eyes. Then his face sagged, and he tried to shake his arm from my grip.

"It's true. I saw him," I hissed. "Out in the woods."

Jobe shifted the jar to his other hand and raised it to his mouth.

"No!" I knocked the poison away from his lips. A wet stain soaked the front of his shirt. He watched it spread.

"Jobe," I said, and shook his shoulder till he looked at me. "Jobe, you didn't kill him."

Still as death, Jobe let me take the jar from his hand. I set it on the table beside the empty crates. Then, like a spell had been broken, my brother, Jobe, and I walked down the aisle and out into the Lexieville night.

≈ *Jobe* ≈

AFTER

Mid-June now, and anything Pert might need there in Little Rock, she's stuffed into a red nylon duffel bag that Joe, from down at Motor Parts, gave her for graduation. He'd also been pleased to be able to offer me full-time work when he heard about Raynell and me getting married.

Back on that awful night, even though Cusper didn't drink his poison, he got sicker than a dog, had some kind of seizure, and Pansy's got him in a rest home in Vernal.

They found Orris the next morning, but he passed on in the hospital emergency room with just Mrs. Turnbull and the sheriff standing by. Orris had caught pneumonia, and no telling what else.

Now it all seems stranger than a dream. But even with our sorrows, now and then for a second I can almost believe we've been touched by the hem of the garment of grace.

Today's the big day for Pert, heading out to Annalene's Coiffure College. Mrs. Turnbull has just driven up, and I'm carrying out the bag, Raynell's hugging Pert, and Lorelei's trying to hand her a sack lunch she packed.

Papa, looking a mix of forlorn and proud, is waiting his turn. He's got on his newest set of white painting clothes for the occasion. I can tell he's going to miss the times we had, the three of us painting together, all filled with hope and laughing about all the different-colored spots we'd dripped on our white hats and in Pert's hair. But them days is over now. Pert and me, we've gone on to better things, just like Papa wanted all along. And now our house has got a painted floor just like Truly planned, and Papa's even started in on the walls.

"Hey, Elwayne," I say when I get outside and see him walking up. Funny how things work out, Elwayne taking my place painting, and all. Papa says he's learning.

"Hey, Jobe," he says, and scuffs his shoes in the dust.

And then we both just stop and watch her at the door, hanging on to Papa like he might be the one going off. They're both crying a little, and when I look round, Mrs. Turnbull is, too.

Raynell, Lorelei, and Elwayne join in. Course, I'm going to miss her more than anybody. There's never been a time I can remember my little sister not being around here. I look up at the clouds passing over for a second.

Pert starts out, then stops there on the upside-down welcome mat, looks down at it, then out at me. We just look awhile, then she's seeing something past me, far out across the road and up into the trees. And Pert's face — well, she looks ready for anything.